Praise for The Bitch

"A very sensual book that gets under your skin. An overwhelming exploration of maternal desire in the beautiful landscapes of Colombia."

LEÏLA SLIMANI

"A searing psychological portrait of a troubled woman contending with her instinct to nurture is at the heart of Colombian writer Quintana's slim, potent English-language debut. The brutal scenes unfold quickly, with lean, stinging prose. Quintana's vivid novel about love, betrayal, and abandonment hits hard."

Publishers Weekly, Starred Review

"The magic of this sparse novel is its ability to talk about many things, all of them important, while seemingly talking about something else entirely. What are those things? Violence, loneliness, resilience, cruelty. Quintana works wonders with her disillusioned, no-nonsense, powerful prose."

JUAN GABRIEL VÁSQUEZ

"A vivid, powerful book, with a tragic core."
Sunday Times

"*The Bitch* is a novel of true violence. Artist that she is, Pilar Quintana uncovers wounds we didn't know we had, shows us their beauty, and then throws a handful of salt into them."
YURI HERRERA

"As Damaris's and Chirli's lives take increasingly tragic turns, their restless natures feel increasingly broadly symbolic of the difficulty of domesticating ourselves and others, even when it serves our best interests. An intense story despite its brevity. A somber and sensitive dog-and-owner tale scrubbed clean of the genre's usual sweetness."
Kirkus Reviews

"Tough and beautiful. The language Quintana uses is concise, sober, ruthless, almost laconic."
HÉCTOR ABAD

"Quintana recreates a wild narrative universe in which the voracity of the jungle, the rain, the sea, and the humidity frame the daily life of the

characters of this short novel. *The Bitch* is one of the most important contemporary novels in Colombia as it broadens the places, voices, and subjectivities from which everyday life, femininity, and motherhood are depicted and narrated."
Latin American Literature Today

"Simply perfect."
MARGARITA GARCÍA ROBAYO, author of *Fish Soup*

"Engrossing. *The Bitch* is a subtle, moving novel about a struggle to overcome loneliness in an eerie place, among memorable people and animals."
Foreword Reviews

"Set in Colombia's Pacific coast, *The Bitch* is a novel that holds the controlled and natural perfection in the narration until the very end."
World Translations Review

"Pilar Quintana's novella manages to tackle, with the lightest of touches, a striking range of profound themes, from poverty and class inequality to loneliness, loss and repentance … This is a wonderfully nuanced meditation on family ties and society's demands, and the central relationship between Damaris and Rogelio is both touchingly tender and grittily believable."

New Internationalist

"*The Bitch* by Colombian writer Pilar Quintana is a devastating portrayal of the aching, unbearable weight that can be felt from guilt, violence, the drive to nurture and the need for human connection."

Shelf Awareness

"This book changes you. It looks deeply into motherhood, cruelty and just how unyielding nature can be, with its wild Colombian coastal landscape, which is as gorgeous as it is brutal. The result is unforgettable."

MARIANA ENRÍQUEZ

"*The Bitch* stands out for the great economy and literary quality of the prose and its ability to display extraordinary oppression amid great openness and geographic immensity. You can read this book without stopping—its story is told in a way that is serene, firm and luminous."

ALONSO CUETO, Jury for the Premio Biblioteca de Narrativa Colombiana

"A perfect novel in its apparent simplicity. A story to be read in one go, in which everything converges in a masterfully described small drama. It seems to be written without effort and flows naturally, leaving behind traces deep and precise, luminous and tremendous."

ANA RODA FORNAGUERA, former director of Colombia's National Library

"Beautifully captures the eerie, wild setting near both the jungle and the ocean. The characters are unforgettable … This is a gorgeous heartbreak of a novel."

Book Riot

"Pilar Quintana's *The Bitch* is a taut, terse tale of guilt, shame, and frustrated desire. Quintana, selected as one of the illustrious Bogotá39 authors in 2007, has crafted a slim, yet powerful story sparse on the prose, yet heavy on the impact. With ample violence and brutality, *The Bitch* lays bare the precipitous emotional and existential toll compounding resentment and failed ambitions inevitably exact. Quintana foregoes literary flourish in favor of a direct, unequivocal style, making her new novel a tough,

even tender take (despite the cruelty) on yearn-
ing, bitterness, regret, and grief."

JEREMY GARBER, Powell's

"This is a book suffused with privation, in which
the jungle is made everyday rather than exoti-
cized, and it's exponentially more powerful for
that. Each of its 155 pages—and its unflinching
ending—are focused on showing us how
Damaris's life is inexorably stripped down to
its bare nerves; language isn't in service of
aesthetics here, but of a surgically precise
excavation of a life at a point of extremis."

Bookmunch

"Pilar Quintana weaves human nature and the
chaos of the universe together with extraordinary mastery. This is a novel full of mysteries
about unfulfilled desire, guilt, and the places
where love still exists."

GABRIELA ALEMÁN, author of *Poso Wells*

"I loved this powerful parable about rage and
disempowerment. There's a vitally important
message contained here about compassion and
transformation, what it means to be a caretaker

for the vulnerable and needy, and who gets acknowledged for their labour in society versus who gets ignored. The class differences are subtly but powerfully captured, and the jungle setting effectively evokes a sticky, sweaty heat. An important story for our times."

JULIANNE PACHICO, author of *The Anthill*

"A raw yet beautiful story about maternity and the jungle."

HAY FESTIVAL

"Compelling to the end."

DAVID HEBBLETHWAITE

"The world of *The Bitch* is heartbreakingly true, it's there, closer than we think, and yet remains invisible."

El País

"Pilar Quintana has created a psychological tale that sweeps and drags us like the waves of the sea."

El Tiempo

"To narrate the baroque jungle and American sea with such sobriety is a great triumph."
Semana

"*The Bitch* is far from simple in its brevity, communicating an inner universe that readers can easily identify with, by having experienced similar circumstances, reliving childhood, or relating to the portrayal of the landscape and those who inhabit it. This novel is a little gem that reminds me, in its intensity and fluidity, of *The Old Man and the Sea* by Hemingway, or *The Pearl* by Steinbeck."
El Nuevo Día

"A profound and moving drama about life and destiny."
WMagazín

"*The Bitch* is a meticulous novel, lugubrious and disquieting as the jungle, and as stifling as the sky described in the book, about to explode."
MELBA ESCOBAR

"A tale narrated with skill and a steady hand."
El Espectador

"*The Bitch* is a chronicle of brutal oppression against women. This novel is chilling, simple, brief, raw—a real literary event."
La Vanguardia

"A powerful text about a woman in revolt who doesn't fully give in to suffering. This short yet intense novel's tour de force is its painting of a sordid violence about to explode at any second."
Le Monde

"A rising voice that affirms itself. Exploring the mysteries of motherhood, this book powerfully questions the temptation of vengeance and death at the cusp of reflecting upon life. In three words: singular, stifling, disquieting."
Lire

"Like Rachel Cusk, Pilar Quintana writes beyond the story. These pages flicker with hope and recurrent violence, shadows cast on and by her protagonist Damaris as she rescues a pup whose fecund, wild nature unearths primordial longing and resentments. Polished down to the line."
KRISTEN MILLARES

"A fierce exploration of maternal desire and of unconditional love, *The Bitch* is a cruel, unforgettable and deeply intelligent story. A big and beautiful discovery."

Page des Libraires

"An extremely sad story that sinks the reader into the main character's emotional void. With an unsparing and laconic style, Pilar Quintana shows that she is one of the most powerful new voices of Latin America."

Deutschlandfunk Kultur

"This work is simple for the reader as far as the narrative is concerned; there are no far-fetched words or technicalities that complicate the reading. However, reading *The Bitch* is not easy at all because of the emotional load that Damaris's life represents, and with it the lives of thousands of women in Colombia and the world who make this fiction a sordid reality, people who ask, shouting, that we recognize them and make visible."

Liberando Letras

"The central relationship of the story allows readers to learn about the harsh history of mistreatment, abandonment, injustice, and heartbreak suffered by the humble and kind Damaris. Thus, enduring the heavy humidity of the jungle that Quintana masterfully portrays, little by little the story makes readers look their own shadows in the eye. Perhaps, in this way, *The Bitch* is a mirror-novel: it invites us to look at what we are not in order to recognize ourselves."
Radio Nacional de Colombia

"Quintana uses language in such a neat way, neat in the sense of its economy, that her novel, in form if not in substance, could be compared to *The Old Man and the Sea*, a work that catapulted Ernest Hemingway. The dogs in Quintana's novel are similar to the dogs in such relevant novels by José Saramago as *The Stone Raft*, *The Cave*, and *Blindness*, works in which dogs become characters, even protagonists—in this sense Quintana's novel is similar to that of the Portuguese writer."
Hecho en Calí

THE BITCH

First edition published in the USA in August 2020 by World Editions
LLC, New York
Second edition published in the USA in October 2020 by World Editions
LLC, New York
Published in the UK in 2020 by World Editions Ltd., London

World Editions
New York/London/Amsterdam

Printed by Lake Book, USA

Library of Congress Cataloging in Publication Data is available

ISBN 978-1-64286-059-7

First published as *La perra* in Colombia in 2017 by Literatura Random
House

This book has been selected to receive financial assistance from English
PEN's PEN Translates programme, supported by Arts Council England.
English PEN exists to promote literature and our understanding of it,
to uphold writers' freedoms around the world, to campaign against the
persecution and imprisonment of writers for stating their views, and
to promote the friendly cooperation of writers and the free exchange of
ideas. www.englishpen.org

Twitter: @WorldEdBooks
Facebook: @WorldEditionsInternationalPublishing
Instagram: @WorldEdBooks
www.worldeditions.org

Book Club Discussion Guides are available on our website.

Pilar Quintana

THE BITCH

Translated from the Spanish
by Lisa Dillman

WORLD EDITIONS

New York, London, Amsterdam

"I FOUND HER there this morning, paws up," said Doña Elodia pointing to the spot on the beach where trash brought in or churned up by the sea collected: branches, plastic bags, bottles.

"Poisoned?"

"I think so."

"What'd you do? Bury her?"

Doña Elodia nodded:

"The grandkids."

"Up in the cemetery?"

"No, right here on the beach."

Plenty of town dogs died by poison. Some people said folks killed them on purpose but Damaris couldn't believe anybody would do such a thing and thought they ate the rat bait people put out by mistake, or maybe they actually ate the rats, which would be easy to catch after they were poisoned.

"I'm sorry," said Damaris.

Doña Elodia just nodded. She'd had that old girl a long time, a black dog that spent all day lying around Doña Elodia's beach restaurant and following her everywhere: to church, her daughter-in-law's, the store, the pier ... She must have been very sad but it didn't show. Setting down one puppy— which she'd just fed with a syringe that she filled from a cup of milk—Doña Elodia picked up another. There were ten in all, and so tiny their eyes hadn't even opened.

"Born six days ago," she said. "They're not going to survive."

Doña Elodia had been old for as long as Damaris could remember, wore thick-lens glasses that made her eyes look buggy, and was fat from the waist down. A woman of few words who moved slow and kept her cool even on the busiest days at the restaurant, when drunks and kids were charging around the outdoor tables. You could tell she was anxious now, though.

"Why don't you give them away?" asked Damaris.

"Somebody took one, but nobody wants pups this young."

Since it was low season, the restaurant had no tables set out on the sand, no music, no tourists, nothing; just empty space that looked enormous, and Doña Elodia on a bench with ten puppies in a cardboard box. Damaris looked them over carefully and made her choice.

"Can I have that one?" she asked.

Doña Elodia set the puppy she'd just fed back in the box, picked up the one Damaris had pointed to—gray fur, floppy ears— and looked behind it.

"It's a girl," she said.

WHEN TIDE WAS out, the beach was massive—a vast expanse of black sand that looked more like mud. When it was in, the water covered the beach completely and the waves brought in twigs, branches, seeds, and dead leaves from the jungle and then churned them all up with people's trash. Damaris was on her way back from visiting her aunt in the next town, which was higher up, on solid ground, and out past the military airport; it was also more modern, with cinder-block hotels and restaurants. She'd stopped at Doña Elodia's out of curiosity after seeing her with the puppies and was now going back to her own place, at the opposite end of the beach. With nowhere to put the puppy, she carried her against her bosom. The tiny dog fit in her hands, smelled of milk, and made Damaris long desperately to hold her tight and cry.

Damaris's town was one long, packed-sand road with houses on either side. All of the houses were rundown, raised up on stilts, and had wood-plank walls and roofs black with mold. Damaris was a little afraid of how Rogelio would react when he saw the dog. He didn't like dogs and only kept them so they'd bark and protect the property. At this point, he had three: Danger, Mosco, and Olivo.

Danger, the oldest, looked like one of those labs the soldiers used for sniffing boats and tourists' suitcases, except his head was big and square like the pitbulls at Hotel Pacífico Real in the next town along. His mother had belonged to the late Josué, a man who had actually liked dogs. Josué also kept them so they'd bark, but he showed them affection too, and trained them to go hunting with him.

According to Rogelio, one day while he was visiting the late Josué, a puppy not two months old broke away from the litter and started barking at him. That, he decided, was the dog for him. The late Josué gave him the dog and Rogelio named him "Danger"—in English. Danger grew up to fulfill the promise of his name, becoming a ferocious and possessive animal. When Rogelio talked about him he seemed to feel respect and admiration, but he never treated him well and was always scaring him, shouting "Gyaaa!" and raising a hand so the dog would remember all the times Rogelio had hit him.

You could tell Mosco had had a hard life as a puppy. He was all small and scrawny and trembly. One day he showed up on the property, and since Danger accepted him, he stayed. When he arrived he had a wound on his tail, and a few days later it got infected. By the time Damaris and Rogelio took any notice of it, the wound was full of maggots and Damaris thought she saw a mosca—a fully formed fly—flutter out of it.

"Did you see that?!" she cried.

Rogelio hadn't seen anything, and when Damaris told him he laughed out loud and said they'd finally found a name for the beast.

"Sit still, Mosco, you son of a bitch," he ordered.

He grabbed the end of the dog's tail, raised his machete, and before Damaris realized what he was doing lopped it off in one go. Mosco took off howling, and Damaris stared at Rogelio in horror. The maggot-ridden tail still in one hand, Rogelio shrugged his shoulders and said he'd only done it to put a stop to the infection. But Damaris always thought he'd enjoyed it.

The youngest dog, Olivo, was the son of Danger and the chocolate lab next door, which the neighbors claimed was purebred. He looked like his father, though his fur was longer and grayer. Olivo was the least friendly of the three. None of them went near Rogelio and they were all wary around people, but Olivo wouldn't even approach anybody and was so distrustful that he wouldn't eat if there were people in sight. Damaris knew that it was because Rogelio, when they were eating, would sometimes creep up to them before they realized and whip them with a thin guadua reed that he kept specifically for this purpose. Sometimes he did it if they'd done something wrong and sometimes just because, just for the pleasure of beating them. Plus Olivo couldn't be trusted: he bit before barking, and from behind.

Damaris told herself things would be different with this dog. This one was hers and she wouldn't let Rogelio do any of those things, wouldn't even let him give the dog dirty looks.

She'd made it to Don Jaime's shop and showed him the puppy.

"What a tiny little thing," he said.

Don Jaime's shop had only one counter and one wall but it was so well stocked you could find anything from food to nails and screws there. Don Jaime was from up-country, had moved to town with nothing back when they were building the naval base and gotten together with a local, a black woman even poorer than him. There were people who said he'd prospered because of his witchcraft, but Damaris thought it was because he was a good man, hard-working too.

That day he gave her a week's vegetables, bread for the next day's breakfast, and a bag of powdered milk and a syringe to feed the puppy, all on credit. He even let her have a cardboard box.

ROGELIO WAS A muscular man, big and black, and his expression made it look like he was always mad. When Damaris got back home with the dog, he was outside cleaning the trimmer's motor. He didn't even say hello.

"Another dog?" he asked. "Don't think I'm going to take care of it."

"You see anybody asking you for anything?" she retorted, and headed straight past him to the shack.

The syringe didn't work. Damaris's arm was strong but clumsy, and her fingers as fat as the rest of her. Every time she pressed the plunger, it went all the way down and the little squirt of milk shot out the dog's mouth and dribbled everywhere. Since the puppy didn't yet know how to lick, she couldn't put milk in a bowl for her, and the only baby bottles they sold in town were for humans—too big. Don Jaime suggested an eyedropper and Damaris gave it a go, but if she had to feed her drop by drop, the dog would never fill her belly. Then Damaris thought of soaking bread in milk and letting the puppy suck at it. That turned out to be the solution: she devoured the whole thing.

The shack where they lived wasn't down on the beach but up on a jungle bluff where white people from the city had big beautiful weekend homes with gardens, paved walkways, and swimming pools. To get from there to town, first you went down a long steep set of steps that had to be scraped often to get the slime off so they wouldn't be slippery. Then you had to cross the cove, a wide inlet where the seawater flowed as fast as a river, filling and emptying with the tides.

Those days high tide was in the morning, so in order to buy the puppy's bread Damaris had to get up first thing, take the paddle from the shack, walk down all the steps with it over her shoulder, push the canoe out from the embarcadero, set it in the water, paddle to the other side, tie it to a palm tree, carry the paddle to one of the fishermen's houses by the cove, ask the fisherman or his wife or his kids to keep an eye on it for her, listen to them complain or gossip about the neighbors, and walk half-way across town to Don Jaime's shop. And the same again on the way back. Every day. Even in the rain.

During the daytime, Damaris carried the little dog around inside her brassiere, between her big soft breasts, to keep her nice and warm. At night she put her in the cardboard box Don Jaime had given her, with a hot-water bottle and the T-shirt she'd worn that day, so the dog wouldn't miss her smell.

The shack where they lived was made of wood and in bad shape. When a storm hit, the whole place shook in the thunder and rocked in the wind, water leaked through the roof and came in through the gaps between wall slats, everything got cold and damp, and the puppy would whimper.

Damaris and Rogelio had slept in separate rooms for ages, so on those nights she leaped quickly out of bed, before he had time to say or do anything. She'd take the dog from the box and stay there in the dark with her, petting her, scared to death of the explosions of lightning and the fury of the wind, feeling tiny—smaller and less significant to the world than a grain of sand in the sea—until the puppy stopped whimpering.

Damaris would pet her during the daytime, too, in the afternoon, once she'd done her morning chores and had lunch, when she sat on a plastic chair to watch her telenovelas with the pup in her lap. If he was there, Rogelio would watch her run her fingers down the dog's back, but he didn't do anything or say anything.

LUZMILA, ON THE other hand, did make comments the day she came to visit, despite the fact that Damaris at no point carried the dog around in her brassiere, instead keeping her in the box as long as she could. Unlike Rogelio, Luzmila didn't hurt animals, but she did revile them and was the type of person who saw the negative side to everything and spent all day criticizing others.

Most of the time, the puppy just slept. When she woke up, Damaris would feed her and put her out on the grass to do her business. During the time Luzmila was there she woke up twice, and both times Damaris fed her and stuck her out on the grass, which was soaking because it had rained all night long and all morning too.

Damaris would have preferred that Luzmila not meet the dog, not even know she had one, but she wasn't going to let her pup go hungry or soil herself. The sky and sea were one solid gray stain and the air so damp that a fish could have lived out of water. Damaris wanted to dry the puppy's paws with a towel and rub her body with her hands to warm the little girl up before setting her back in the box, but she stopped herself since Luzmila kept staring at her with those evil eyes of hers.

"You're going to kill that animal, you keep touching it so much," she said.

Damaris was hurt by the comment, but she kept quiet. It wasn't worth a fight. Then, wearing her disgusted face, Luzmila asked what the dog's name was, and Damaris had to tell her: Chirli. They were first cousins and had been raised together since birth, so they knew everything about one another.

"Chirli, like the beauty queen?" Luzmila laughed. "Isn't that what you were going to name your daughter?"

Damaris had been unable to have children. She and Rogelio got together when she was eighteen, and when she'd been with him for two years people started saying "Where are the babies?" and "Sure taking your time." They were doing nothing to prevent a pregnancy so Damaris started drinking infusions made from mountain herbs—María and Espíritu Santo—that people said were very good for fertility.

Back then they lived in town, in a rented apartment, and she would walk up to gather the herbs on the bluff without asking permission from the property owners. Though it felt a little dishonest, she considered it her business and no one else's. She prepared and drank the infusions secretly, while Rogelio was out fishing or hunting.

He began to suspect Damaris was up to something and one day trailed her like an animal he was hunting, without her realizing. When Rogelio saw the herbs he thought they were for witchcraft and confronted her, furious.

"What are you doing with this shit?!" he asked. "What are you up to?"

It was drizzling outside. They were deep in the jungle, in an ugly spot where the trees had been felled for electricity cables to get through. The rotting trunks, still standing, looked like untended graves in a cemetery. Rogelio was in swamp boots but she, barefoot, had mud-covered feet. Damaris hung her head and, in a quiet voice, told him the truth. He stood in silence for a spell.

"I'm your husband," he said finally, "you're not in this alone."

From then on, they gathered the herbs together, made the infusions together, and at night argued over what names they'd give their children. Since they couldn't agree on any, not a single one, they decided that he would choose the boys' and she the girls'. They wanted four, ideally two of each. But two more years went by and then they had to tell anyone who asked that she just wasn't getting pregnant. People started to avoid the topic and Aunt Gilma suggested Damaris go see Santos.

Though it was a man's name, Santos was not a man but the daughter of a black woman from Chocó and an indigenous man from lower San Juan. She knew herbs, and could heal by touch—rubbing people's bodies—and by secrets—invoking words and prayers. She tried a little of everything on Damaris and when it all failed said the problem must be her husband, and to bring him in. Though it was clear he was uneasy about the whole thing, Rogelio drank all the potions, accepted all the prayers, and put up with all of Santos's rubbing. But the longer they went without her getting pregnant the more reluctant he became, and one day he announced he wasn't going back. Damaris took this as a personal attack and stopped speaking to him.

Though they continued to live together, and to sleep in the same bed, they went three months without speaking. Then one night, Rogelio came home a little drunk and told her that he wanted a child too, he just didn't want the pressure of Santos and her goddam herbs and prayers and rubs. But he was there for her, and if Damaris wanted, they could keep trying. The room they shared at the time was the storeroom of a big house that had long since stopped being the nicest in town. It was in a sorry state now, full of termites and grime, and their room was so narrow it hardly fit the bed, their old box TV, and a two-burner gas cooktop. But it did have a window overlooking the sea.

Damaris stood a while at the window just feeling the rust-smelling breeze on her face. When Rogelio finished getting undressed and climbed into bed, she closed the window, lay down next to him, and began to stroke him. That night they had sex without fretting about children or anything else, and from then on they didn't talk about it anymore—though sometimes when she heard about an acquaintance getting pregnant or a child born in town, Damaris cried silent tears, scrunching up her eyes and fists, after he fell asleep.

When Damaris turned thirty they were doing a little better and had moved to a slightly larger room in the same house. She was working at one of the houses up on the bluff—Señora Rosa's place—which meant she earned a fixed salary, and Rogelio went out fishing on what people called "wind-and-tides"—boats that spent days on end at high sea and could carry tons of fish. On one trip, Rogelio and his partner caught three grouper, loads of sierra, and found an entire shoal of red snapper they could take—almost a ton and a half in total—so they each made loads of cash. Though he wanted to use it to buy a new drift net and a huge four-speaker sound system, Damaris had been wondering for some time how to say she hadn't stopped hoping for a child and wanted to try again, no matter what sacrifices they had to make.

Aunt Gilma had told her about a woman who was thirty-eight, far older than her, who'd managed to get pregnant, and now, with the assistance of a jaibaná—an indigenous doctor who was famous in the next town—had a beautiful baby. His consultations weren't cheap, but with the money they'd saved they could start treatment. And then they'd see. The night Rogelio announced that he was going to Buenaventura the next day to buy the stereo, Damaris cried.

"I don't want a stereo," she said, "I want a baby."

Sobbing, she told him about the thirty-eight-year-old, about all the times she'd cried silently, about how awful it was that everyone in town could have babies except her, about the stabbing pain she got in her soul every time she saw a pregnant woman or a newborn or a couple with a child, about the sheer torture of always longing for a little baby she could hold and rock against her bosom, only to get her period every month. Rogelio listened without a word, and then he embraced her. They were in bed at the time, so it was a full-body embrace, and that's how they fell asleep.

The jaibaná treated Damaris for a long time. He gave her potions and baths, invited her to ceremonies where he anointed her, rubbed her, blew smoke at her, prayed for her, chanted to her. Then he did the same to Rogelio, who this time didn't have a bad attitude or give up. And this was all just preparation. The actual treatment was to be an operation he'd give Damaris, but without opening her up anywhere, an operation that would cleanse the paths that her egg and Rogelio's sperm needed to travel and prepare her womb to receive the child. It cost a lot, and they had to save a whole year to pay for it.

The operation took place one night at the jaibaná's clinic, which was a thatched-roof hut on very high stilts out past the next town, in the middle of a barren hill whose trees had been felled, a hill teeming with biting midges, brushland, prickly ferns, and grasses that grew together and tangled over each other. Damaris and Rogelio said goodbye outside the hut, because nobody but her and the jaibaná were allowed to be present.

Once they were alone, the jaibaná gave her a dark bitter liquid to drink and told her to lie on the floor, on top of a mattress. She was wearing knee-length leggings and a short-sleeved blouse, and the second she lay down she was attacked by a cloud of midges that left the jaibaná alone but bit her all over, even her ears and her scalp and through her clothes. Then suddenly they disappeared and Damaris heard an owl hooting in the distance. The owl's call slowly grew closer and when it got so loud that this was the only thing she could hear, Damaris fell asleep.

She didn't feel anything else, and the next day woke up with all her clothes intact, the same dull ache in her back as ever and nothing about her body feeling different. Rogelio was waiting for her outside and took her home.

Damaris wasn't even late that month, and the jaibaná said there was nothing else he could do for them. In a way it was a relief, since having sex had become a burden. They stopped having it, at first maybe just as a break, and she felt freed but at the same time crushed and inadequate, a disgrace as a woman, a freak of nature.

By that time they were living on the bluff. Their shack had a small living room, two narrow rooms, a bathroom with no shower, and a counter with no sink where they could have put a stove, though instead they chose to cook outside in the gazebo, which was large and had a big sink and a wood fire, meaning they could save on the cost of gas cylinders. The shack was tiny; Damaris could clean the whole place in under two hours. But she threw herself into her chores so obsessively during those days that it took a week. She scrubbed the wall planks inside and out, the top as well as the underside of the floorboards, used a toothbrush to scrape gunk from between the joints, a nail to dig out anything in the holes and grooves in the wood, and cleaned the inside of the sheet-metal roof with a sponge. In order to accomplish all of this she had to climb on a plastic chair, on the kitchen counter, and on the toilet tank, which, since it was ceramic, broke beneath her weight and then they had to save to replace it.

Two months later, when Rogelio reached for Damaris again, she rejected him, and the following night she rejected him again, and on like this for a week until he stopped trying. Damaris was glad. She no longer fooled herself about the possibility of getting pregnant, no longer waited anxiously for her period not to come, no longer suffered when it did. But he, bitter or resentful, began to reprimand her for breaking the toilet tank, and every time anything

—a plate, a jar, a glass—slipped from her hands, which was often, he criticized and mocked her. "Butterfingers," he said, "you think dishes grow on trees?" "Next time I'm charging you, you hear me?" One night, on the pretext that he was snoring and keeping her awake, Damaris moved to the other room and never came back.

Now here she was about to turn forty, the age women dry up, as she'd once heard Tío Eliécer say. Not long before, the day she adopted the puppy, Luzmila had straightened her hair, and as she was applying the straightener she admired Damaris's skin, which was in great shape and had no wrinkles or dark spots.

"Look at me, on the other hand," she said, and by way of explanation added, "Course, you didn't have kids."

Luzmila had been in a good mood that day and was simply trying to pay a compliment, but it cut Damaris to the quick, this realization that her cousin, and no doubt everyone else, thought that hers was a lost cause; and it was, she knew, but it was still hard to accept.

So this new comment from her cousin, who at thirty-seven had two daughters and two granddaughters, gave her the urge to be dramatic, like the people on TV novelas, and say—tears in her eyes, so Luzmila would lament her cruelty—"Yes, I named her Chirli, like the daughter I never had." But she didn't get dramatic, didn't say anything at all. She took the puppy back to the box and asked her cousin if that week she'd spoken to her father, Tío Eliécer, who lived in the south and had been feeling poorly of late.

SOMETIMES WHEN SHE went down to town, Damaris stopped in at Doña Elodia's to ask after the puppies. Doña Elodia had kept one for herself, which she kept at the restaurant in the cardboard box and still fed with the syringe. She'd managed to give the others away to acquaintances in one of the two towns, but day by day the pups were dying. One, because the main dog at its new house attacked it; the other seven, no one knew why. Damaris tried to tell herself it was because they were too delicate and people didn't know how to take care of them, but Luzmila's words rang out in her head, over and over: "You're going to kill that animal, you keep touching it so much," and she thought perhaps she, too, was doing it all wrong and that one of these days the little doggie would wake up dead, stiff as her siblings.

By the end of the first month, only three of the eleven puppies were still alive: the girl Damaris had taken, the boy Doña Elodia had kept, and another one taken by Ximena, a woman of about sixty who made a living selling handicrafts in the next town. Damaris was surprised Ximena's dog hadn't died. She barely knew the woman, but knew she didn't lead a good life. Once, during the festival of the whales, she'd seen Ximena so drunk she couldn't stand; and another time, a Sunday morning it was, she found her passed out drunk on the steps leading down to the beach in the next town, vomit stains on her clothes.

"Ours are out of danger now," Doña Elodia said. "If any of them dies, it'll be of something else."

Damaris was overcome, first by relief and then by satisfaction at it being Luzmila and not her who was wrong, though she wouldn't throw it in her cousin's face. Luzmila felt attacked by every single thing Damaris said and got mad about everything. Why cause trouble when the pup, who'd opened her eyes some time ago and now walked to her food bowl on her own, would be the one to prove her right?

Damaris still carried the little dog around in her brassiere, but set her down on the ground for longer each day because she was getting heavier and heavier. The pup had learned how to lick, to feed from the bowl, to eat the fish soup Damaris made her from scraps, and, in the past few days, she even ate leftovers, like the other dogs. Plus, Damaris was teaching her to do her business outside the hut and the gazebo where they spent their mornings, Damaris cooking and folding clean clothes.

Thus far, Rogelio had left the little dog alone. But now that she was more energetic and followed Damaris everywhere, jumping, attacking her feet, and tormenting the other dogs with her sharp little teeth, Damaris was on guard. If Rogelio did anything at all, if he dared to so much as raise a hand to the dog, she'd kill him. But all he did was tell her it was time to start keeping the pup outside. They couldn't have her getting used to being with people all the time and then go and destroy something at the big house.

TÍO ELIÉCER HAD owned the bluff until the seventies, when he divided it into four lots and put them up for sale. He had raised Damaris, because the man who got her mother pregnant—a soldier doing his military service in the region—abandoned her when she got knocked up, and in order to support her daughter she had to work as a live-in, keeping house for a family in Buenaventura. She sent money whenever she could and came back for Christmas, Semana Santa, and sometimes for long weekends. Damaris was raised in a shack that Tío Eliécer and Tía Gilma owned, on the land that now belonged to Señora Rosa—the first lot they sold. They sold the adjacent land next, to an engineer from the city of Armenia, and the lot behind it to the Reyes family.

The Reyes family was made up of Señor Luis Alfredo, who was from Cali but lived in Bogotá; his wife Elvira, who was from Bogotá; and their son Nicolasito. They had a big house built entirely of sheet metal—the most modern construction material at the time—with a pool and a large gazebo that had a sink and a wood-fire grill where they could make sancocho and asado and have parties. And a wooden shack for the caretakers. Damaris's family moved onto the plot that hadn't yet sold, which bordered the Reyeses'. Because the Reyes family spent all their vacations there, Nicolasito and Damaris became friends. They were the same age and born on the same day, a terrible day for a birthday: January 1.

It was December. The town still didn't have electricity back then, Shirley Sáenz was crowned the new Miss Colombia, and Damaris and Luzmila spent ages admiring her in the *Cromos* magazines Señora Elvira brought up from Bogotá. Nicolasito used to pretend he was an explorer and organize expeditions on the bluff, expeditions on which Damaris acted as guide and they carried flashlights even though it was day-time. They were about to turn eight. Most of the time Luzmila went with them, but that day she threw a hissy fit when they said she couldn't lead the expedition, flung to the ground the stick she carried to fend off snakes, and went home whining.

Damaris and Nicolasito made it to their destination, a low rocky headland where the waves licked at the bluff. At first they were transfixed, watching leafcutter ants descend a tree single file, transporting pieces of foliage. They were big, red and hard, with pointy things on their heads and bodies. "It looks like they're wearing armor," Nicolasito said. Then he walked over to the rocks, saying he wanted to feel the spray of the waves on his face. Damaris tried to stop him, explained that it was dangerous, told him that the rocks there were slippery and the sea treacherous. But he didn't listen and went and stood on the rocks, and the wave that crashed just then, a violent wave, carried him off.

The image remained engraved in Dama-ris's mind: a tall, white boy standing face to the sea, followed by the white crest of the wave, and then nothing—empty rocks above a green sea, which looked calm in the distance. And her, there by the leafcutter ants, unable to do a thing.

Damaris had to return alone, through a jungle that seemed denser and darker than ever. The treetops above her formed a solid canopy, and the roots below snarled together. Her feet sank into the dead leaves carpeting the ground and got buried in the mud, and she began to feel like the breathing she could hear was not her own but that of the jungle, and that it was she and not Nicolasito who was drowning in a green sea full of leafcutters and foliage. She wanted to run away, get lost, say nothing to anyone, be swallowed up by the jungle. She started to run, tripped and fell, got up and ran again.

When Damaris reached the Reyeses' property, she found Tía Gilma inside the shack, talking to the caretakers. Tía Gilma listened to what Damaris recounted, didn't utter a single word of reproach, and took charge of everything. She asked the caretakers to go out in the canoe to search for Nicolasito and went to tell Señora Elvira what had happened herself. Señor Luis Alfredo was out deep-sea fishing, so Señora Elvira was alone at the house. Tía Gilma went inside and Damaris stayed outside on the veranda. There was no wind. The leaves on the trees were still and the only sound was that of the sea. To Damaris it felt as if time was stretching, as if she would be there on the veranda until she grew up and then grew old.

Finally they emerged. Señora Elvira was like a crazy person. She shouted, sobbed, crouched down to Damaris, stood up, paced the veranda, gesticulated, asked a question and then another one, and then asked the same thing again in a slightly different way. Damaris no longer remembered what it was she asked, but did remember her face, and the anguish in her eyes, which were blue with the little veins burst and blood staining the whites.

That day they searched for Nicolasito until nightfall and kept searching tirelessly every day after that. Tío Eliécer was helping with the search and, in the afternoons, when he came back with the bad news, he'd sit on a tree trunk by the door to the shack. Damaris knew that this was the sign for her to approach. She did so without dawdling, as she didn't want him to get any madder than he already was. Then her uncle would grab a hard, flexible switch cut from a guayaba tree and whip her. Tía Gilma had told her not to tense up, that the more she relaxed her thighs, which was where her uncle struck her, the less it would hurt. She tried, but fear and the cracking of the first lash made her clench every muscle tight, and each new blow hurt more than the last. Her thighs looked like the back of Christ. The first day he'd given her one lash, the second two, and so on, adding one for each day Nicolasito didn't turn up.

Tío Eliécer stopped on the day that he would have given her thirty-four lashes. Thirty-four days had gone by, longer than the sea had ever taken to return a body. The skin had decomposed from the salt and sun, been eaten down to the bone by fish in some places, and, according to those who were there, the body reeked.

Tía Gilma, Luzmila, and Damaris went to the bluff to watch. A body that now looked smaller, the tiny body of a boy, there on the sand, and Señora Elvira, so blonde, so thin, so pretty, lifting it up a little in order to embrace her son and cover him in kisses as though he were still handsome. Tía Gilma put her arm around Damaris, and then Damaris couldn't take it anymore and burst into tears for the first time since the tragedy.

THE REYESES DIDN'T return to their house
on the bluff but didn't put it up for sale
either. Tío Eliécer sold the last of his lots to
two sisters from Tuluá, had a two-story
house built in town, and moved in there
with his family and Damaris's mother,
who was no longer working in Buenaventura. This was a time of plenty. With his
earnings from the first sales, her uncle
bought land in the south—where the children he'd had with his first wife went to
live—and two boats, which he rented out
for fishing. He'd suddenly become well-
to-do and threw parties that lasted all
weekend long and took up the whole block.
That was how his money started to disappear.

Tío Eliécer ended up in so much debt

that he had to sell one of his boats to pay it off. Then came a run of bad luck. The following year, the second boat sank in rough waters, and a few months later, during the December celebrations, Damaris's mother got hit in the chest by a stray bullet. Since they could do nothing for her at the medical post in town, she was transported to the emergency room in Buenaventura by lifeboat, but by the time they got to the hospital she had died. Damaris, who was about to turn fifteen, canceled her party. She and her mother had been planning it together, and now all she wanted was to cry in peace in the room she shared with Luzmila. Her cousin sat beside her on the bed, braiding tiny cornrows into Damaris's hair and reporting all the local gossip until she managed to make her laugh.

The townspeople said this much misfortune wasn't normal, that it must be the work of some spite-filled wretch who'd put a curse on them. Troubled, her aunt and uncle called on Santos, who did a cleansing of the house and every member of the family, but things did not improve.

Rough tides knocked their house down and, having no money to rebuild, the family split up. By that time Rogelio had come to town on a broken-down fishing boat. While awaiting spare parts from Buenaventura, and then waiting for the boat to be fixed, he spent his days drinking beer and watching girls in town. He met Damaris one Sunday on the beach and, when the boat was ready, he quit his job and rented a room in town, and Damaris went with him. Tío Eliécer and Tía Gilma separated. He went to live in the south with his older children and she got a job as a waitress at Hotel Pacífico Real and moved to the next town with Luzmila.

In time the Reyeses stopped raising the caretakers' salaries or sending them the products needed to maintain the property —detergent, fertilizer, wax, insecticide, paint, bleach, oil, and gas for the trimmer and pool treatment system. Then people found out that their business in Bogotá—a suitcase factory—had gone bankrupt. The caretakers quit when they got jobs on an inland estate, and Josué agreed to look after the Reyeses' house. He'd just moved to town and had no wife, no children, and nothing to lose. They paid him less than half of minimum wage, but he made up for it by fishing and hunting. One day the Reyeses just stopped paying him, and he stayed on at the property because he had no place to go. But some time later he died of a shotgun blast, in what seemed to be a hunting accident.

Tío Eliécer was living in the south, Tía Gilma had suffered a stroke and was hard to understand when she spoke, and Luzmila, who was now married, had just given birth to her second daughter in Buenaventura. Aside from Damaris, there was no one left in town who'd been close to the Reyeses and could let them know of Josué's death.

Cell phones had yet to make it to the region back then. The Telecom office was located between the two towns and was one of the few brick buildings around. It had only one window, so when it was hot out, it was hotter in, and if it was a chilly day, it was even chillier inside. Damaris had never been to Bogotá, or even to Cali. The only city she knew was Buenaventura, which was an hour away by boat and had no big buildings. She didn't know the cold of the mountains either, but based on what she saw on TV and what people said, she pictured Bogotá like the Telecom office after a week of rains: a dark place, full of echoes and smelling of damp, like a cave.

The day she called the Reyeses it was sunny out, but there were lots of clouds and it was so muggy in town it was like being in a pot of sancocho. Damaris's hands were sweating and the little slip of paper where she'd written the phone number—which she'd gotten from one of the late Josué's notebooks—almost dissolved. She went into the phone booth and dialed the number; the call took a second too long to connect and as she listened to the phone ring it struck Damaris that on the other end of that sound was a very ugly part of her past and a monstrous city that she couldn't picture. She was about to hang up when a man answered.

"Señor Luis Alfredo?"

"Yes."

Damaris wanted to run.

"This is Damaris."

Señor Luis Alfredo heard the name and then came an awful silence, which she accepted with resignation just as she'd accepted the lashes her uncle had given her each afternoon for thirty-three days. To the Reyeses she was a black crow, a sign of bad luck. Then, as best she could, anxiously, she told him what had happened: two days earlier a shotgun blast had been heard out on the bluff. Her husband and some other men from town went up to look for Josué, but didn't find him in the shack or on the trails. The following day the turkey vultures were circling the bluff and led them to the body.

"Suicide," Señor Luis Alfredo said in shock.

"No, I don't think so, sir. I spoke to him last week and he didn't seem poorly, wasn't sad or anything."

"Oh."

"Even had plans to go to Buenaventura and buy some boots he needed."

"Oh."

"And my husband says maybe he just fell and the shotgun went off. The body was in the scrub, in a very strange position."

"Your husband?"

"Yes, sir."

"You're thirty-three now, is that right?"

There came another awful silence and then Damaris replied, as though apologizing:

"Yes, sir."

Señor Luis Alfredo sighed. Then he said he was sorry about the caretaker's death, thanked Damaris for calling, and asked if she could take charge of the property.

"You know how important it is to us."

"Yes, sir."

"I'll send you your salary and supplies."

Damaris knew that this wasn't true but acted as though she believed him and said yes to everything. It wasn't just that she felt indebted to the Reyeses, she was also excited at the idea of going back to live on the bluff, which she'd always considered her home.

Rogelio wasn't hard to convince. They

wouldn't have to pay any rent on the bluff, and even though the caretakers' shack wasn't much, it was bigger than the room they had in town, plus they could fix it up. In order to support themselves they'd keep working as they had until now, with him hunting in the jungle and fishing on wind-and-tides and her at Señora Rosa's, where she was needed now more than ever since Señor Gene, her husband, had been confined to a wheelchair.

The one thing they didn't like was that the Reyes property had no electricity. But Señora Rosa's, which was just opposite, did, and she gave Damaris and Rogelio permission to run an extension cord from the transformer at her house so they could have light. They brought their things—the old box TV, the gas stove they never used, the bed and sheets Tía Gilma had given them—and settled in more comfortably at the shack than they ever had at their room in town.

Working on the Reyeses' property wasn't complicated. To do the laundry and cleaning, they used the same products they were already buying for the shack anyway; they kept the pool empty and washed it when it rained; they fertilized the garden with compost they got from the jungle; and Rogelio cut the grass with the gas that was left over from his fishing trips. The big house could have done with a fresh coat of paint and having its cracked slats replaced, and the walkways were in need of repair where the pavement had rotted, but they kept everything clean and well maintained. When the Reyeses came back, they would have nothing to complain about.

THE CARETAKERS WHO'D worked for the Reyeses did so convinced that at some point the couple would return to the place where their son had died. So they'd all taken pains to keep the house—the late Nicolasito's room, especially—just as the Reyeses had left it, to the degree that the climate, jungle, salt, and the passage of time allowed.

The big house had been built to withstand the harshest conditions. The aluminum siding was rust-proof, the floor made of Brazilian cherry—a very fine hardwood resistant to termites and weevils—and for the foundation and elevated slab they'd used a special, stronger cement mix. Rather than attractive, the house was practical, with wide open spaces and furniture made of synthetic materials. The late Nicolasito's room was the only one that had been decorated. Señora Elvira had special-ordered his bed and wardrobe from the best carpenter in town and painted it bright colors herself. The curtains and bedding she'd brought from Bogotá: a matching set, with *Jungle Book* motifs. They were a little faded now and had a few holes, but only very tiny ones and from a distance you couldn't tell. In the wardrobe, sprinkled with mothballs, some of Nicolasito's clothes remained: a few T-shirts and pants, two pairs of swim trunks, tennis shoes, and some flip-flops. The door was propped open with a conch he'd brought back from a trip to Negritos reef one day when he went out fishing with his father, and his toys were kept in a wooden chest that Señora Elvira had also painted. Those made of plastic or wood had survived; the ones with metal parts had rusted years ago.

Damaris now accepted that Rogelio was right. She couldn't let the dog get used to being with her in the shack or the big house, where she spent much of her time cleaning and waxing. She might destroy something: the late Nicolasito's conch or one of his toys, his tennis shoes or, God forbid, the furniture his mother had painted.

With sorrow and guilt, Damaris left the dog outside the shack and stopped letting her follow her into either of the two houses, which were raised off the ground on stakes—special cement ones for the big house and ordinary wood ones for the shack. But nor did she force the little dog to live under the houses with the other three. Instead, she gave her a special spot in the gazebo, where the other dogs were not allowed and she'd be protected from the rain.

IT WAS TÍA Gilma's birthday and Damaris set out early to go see her, before the first boats from Buenaventura docked. Summer high season had started that day, and she wanted to avoid the hordes of tourists who would land at the pier and go to the next town, which was where the better hotels were.

The night before it had only drizzled lightly. The morning sky was clear and the sea very calm. You could tell it was going be one of those rare cloudless days when it was burning hot, with bright blue sky. When she passed Doña Elodia's place, Doña Elodia came out and waved to Damaris. Her daughters were setting out tables at the restaurant and putting on tablecloths. Doña Elodia was wearing her apron, a fish-gutting knife in one hand.

"Ximena's dog died," she said.

Damaris was taken aback.

"How?" she asked.

"Poisoned, she says."

"Like his mother."

Doña Elodia nodded.

"Just yours and mine left now," she said.

The pups had made it to six months. Doña Elodia's was lying on the sand outside the restaurant, same place his mother used to do. He was medium-sized, like Damaris's, but that was their only likeness. His ears were pointy and his fur black and scraggly, whereas her puppy's ears had stayed floppy and her fur was still gray, very short. No one would have guessed they came from the same litter. Damaris had the urge to go back home to hug her puppy and make sure she was okay, but it was Tía Gilma's birthday and she forced herself to keep going, to the next town.

Tía Gilma had trouble moving around since her stroke and spent all her time in a rocker they moved back and forth, from the living room to the entry hall, the entry hall to the living room. She slept in a room with Luzmila's two daughters and her granddaughters. The older daughter's husband worked in Buenaventura and only came back on the odd weekend. Luzmila and her husband slept in the other room. He worked construction and she sold stuff out of catalogs: clothes, perfume, make-up, hair straighteners, pots and pans ... They were doing alright. The house was small, but it was made of brick and they had furniture: an oval dining-room table made from wood, and two floral-print sofas in the living room.

They had shrimp and rice for lunch, sang happy birthday, and ate a cake with blue frosting that had been ordered from Buenaventura. The girls gave their great-grandmother a gift and tears slid down her face. Damaris placed an arm around her and rubbed her back for a while. Then the girls insisted on playing with their Tía Damaris and climbed up her legs and arms. The door and all of the windows were open, but the sun was high in the sky and there was no hint of a breeze. Luzmila and her

daughters fanned themselves with catalogs, Tía Gilma rocked slowly in her chair,
and the girls kept jumping on Damaris,
who began to feel suffocated.

"Not now," she said to them, "Time to
stop, please."

But the girls wouldn't stop, not until
Luzmila yelled at them and sent them to
their room.

In the afternoon, on the way back to her
own town, Damaris passed the handicraft
stalls. Tourists were still arriving from the
pier—on foot or by moto-taxi, bags over
their shoulders, tired and sweaty—but
most had already settled in to their hotels
and lots of them were now out wandering
around, looking at the werregue-palm bas-
kets and manicaria-palm hats and bags
that the indigenous vendors displayed on
faded sheets on the ground. It was hard to
make her way through all the people.

At one point, Damaris got trapped in
front of Ximena's spot, which was much
nicer than those of the indigenous. Hers
was a stall, raised off the ground with a
plastic roof, and the display board she used

for her merchandise was covered in blue velvet. She sold bracelets, necklaces, rings, earrings, woven wristbands, and rice paper and pipes for marijuana. Damaris and Ximena exchanged glances and Ximena got up and rushed over to her.

"They killed my little dog," she said.

The two of them had never spoken.

"Doña Elodia told me."

"It was the neighbors, those sons of bitches."

Damaris was uncomfortable hearing them spoken of this way, even though she didn't know the people, but at the same time felt sorry for Ximena. She smelled of marijuana and had a hoarse smoker's voice, sunspots on her wrinkled skin, and you could see the white roots of her hair, which was long and dyed black. Ximena told her that a few weeks ago a chicken belonging to the neighbors had crossed the fence and her dog killed it while it was on Ximena's property, and now, mysteriously, the dog turned up dead. Beyond this, she had no further proof against the neighbors and couldn't even be sure the dog had actually been poisoned. Damaris thought maybe he'd died of something else—a snake bite or a disease, say—and that Ximena was only this furious with the neighbors as a way to keep from plunging into sadness.

"I wanted a girl dog," she admitted, "but Doña Elodia told me you got the only one in the litter, so I took him instead. He was so tiny, remember what they looked like? My little Simoncito fit in my hands."

WHEN SHE GOT home, Damaris was as happy to see the dog as the dog was her, and she petted her for a long time and only stopped after looking down at her hands and seeing they were covered in filth. She decided to give her a bath. The sun was still beating down and Damaris needed to rinse off the heat and sweat of her walk. She bathed the pup in the washtub using the blue laundry soap and brush, much to the displeasure of the little dog, who hated water and lowered her head and hid her tail.

Afterward, as the dog was drying in the last rays of sun, Damaris washed some underwear she'd left to soak and then bathed herself as well. Since the shack had no shower they always bathed in the washtub without taking off their clothes, using a totuma gourd to pour water over their bodies. The late afternoon was spectacular. The sky looked like it was on fire and the sea turned purple. Night was falling by the time she hung the underwear out on a small drying rack she kept in the gazebo and placed the dog, still affronted after the bath, in her bed—a small mat folded in two that Damaris had covered with old towels.

That night it still hadn't rained, but they had to close the door and every window in the shack because the clavitos—tiny mosquitos that bit like pinpricks—were in a frenzy. Rogelio went for a banged-up old pot they kept under the house, filled it with coconut jute, and set it alight. The jute started to burn and the clavitos disappeared for a little while, but no sooner had the smoke cleared than the bugs came back in strength, and they both had to use rags to fend them off. They couldn't watch the novela in peace. It was so hot that Rogelio had sweat stains under his arms, and a stream of water ran down Damaris's sideburns.

"Isn't it ever going to rain?" she complained, waving her rag.

Rogelio said nothing in reply and went off to his bed. She stayed up watching TV, knowing that with this heat and the clavitos torturing her she'd never be able to fall asleep.

After midnight, when the infomercials came on, a single flash of lightning suddenly exploded, so close that for a second everything lit up. Damaris jumped in fright, the lights went out, and a torrential downpour began, with lightning, thunder, and so much rain it was as if buckets of water were being dumped onto the roof. But the air cooled, the clavitos disappeared, and Damaris, knowing the dog was safe in the gazebo, went to bed.

The following morning it was still raining hard, and since she'd been awake all night, Damaris got up late. The ground was cold and wet and the pot where they'd burned the coconut jute the night before was now in the middle of the living room catching water from a leak. The power hadn't come back on and Rogelio was sitting in one of the plastic chairs in front of the darkened TV, drinking coffee he must have made in the gazebo.

"Dog of yours made a mess last night," he said.

Damaris grew alarmed, not at whatever it was the dog might have done but at the punishment Rogelio must have given her in Damaris's absence.

"What did you do to her?"

"Me? I didn't do shit. But she ripped your bras to shreds."

Damaris rushed out to the gazebo. She couldn't see the sea, the islands, the town—nothing but the rain, white as a gauze curtain in the distance, running like a river down the roofs, walkways, and steps throughout the property. Damaris was drenched when she got to the gazebo. Her panties and Rogelio's undershorts, which she'd hung on the clothes rack the night before, were still in place. Only her bras, three of them, lay on the floor, shredded. The dog wagged her tail timidly, guiltily, but looked fine. Damaris examined her head and tail, and such was her relief at finding the dog safe and sound that rather than a scolding she gave her a hug and told her it was okay, that she got the message and would never give her another bath, ever again.

DAMARIS CONTINUED TO pamper the dog until she ran off and got lost in the jungle. It happened one night when Damaris was on her own, Rogelio had gone out fishing on a wind-and-tide. Danger, Olivo, and Mosco had just eaten by the gazebo and Damaris was rubbing her pup's head goodnight, about to go into the shack. Suddenly Danger started barking in the direction of the jungle. The other two dogs went on the alert and then hers came out of the gazebo and trotted the few meters over to Danger's side. There were no houses or people in the direction they were barking, so Damaris assumed it was an animal—an opossum, a hedgehog, or a peccary that was lost or sick. Since there was no moon it was extremely dark, the only light coming from the bare bulb in the gazebo. She couldn't see or hear anything in the distance, but the dogs were getting more and more het up, hackles raised and barking furiously.

Damaris started calling the pup in an attempt to calm her down and get her to come back. "Chirli!" she yelled, for once not ashamed to say the name that her cousin had mocked out loud. "Chiiiiirliiiii!" But suddenly Danger bolted and they all followed, even her dog, who took off into the jungle with them.

Damaris could hear them barking and moving around in the underbrush. Given that she was barefoot and it could be a snake—most likely a lancehead: nocturnal, and vicious, and poisonous—all she could do was keep calling from the gazebo. She tried different voices—furious, neutral, sweet, imploring—with no luck, and then everything went quiet and she could no longer hear any barking or anything at all. Before her lay nothing but jungle, still as a beast that's just swallowed its prey.

Damaris went into the shack, put on her swamp boots, grabbed the machete and flashlight, and headed for the jungle the same way the dogs had gone. At no point did she feel afraid of any of the things in the jungle she was afraid of: the dark, the lanceheads, the wild animals, the dead, Nicolasito and Josué and Señor Gene, the ghosts people talked about when she was a girl. Damaris was not surprised by her bravery. She had only one thought: the pup was in danger and she had to save her.

She was walking through the undergrowth without going too far in so as not to get lost in the dark, shining the light in every direction, making noise and calling to her pup, and to Danger, Olivo, and Mosco. When none of them came back and nothing happened, she decided to venture further in. She went to the gully separating the Reyeses' property from the neighbors', to the fence by the main road, out onto the bluff, and as far as the milpesos palms where the only trail out that way came to an end.

Damaris could only see whatever she aimed the flashlight at, parts of things—a huge leaf, a tree trunk carpeted in moss, the wing of an enormous moth covered in eyes and surprised by the light, which took flight and then fluttered in panic around her head. Her boots got caught in the roots and sank into the mud, she stumbled and slipped, and, to keep her footing, put her hands against surfaces that were hard, or wet, or coarse. Things brushed against her, things that were rough, hairy, prickly, and she startled, thinking that they were a spider, a tree snake, a blood-sucking bat; but nothing bit her except for the mosquitos, and she didn't care and kept searching in the dark. The heat was so muggy that she felt it sticking to her skin like slime and it was as if the cacophony of frogs and crickets—as unbearable as the music at the disco in the next town—came not from the jungle but from inside her head. The flashlight started to dim and she had no choice but to return to the shack, weeping and defeated, before it went all the way out.

Damaris fell asleep instantly, but her dream left her feeling she'd had no rest. She dreamed of noises and shadows, that she was awake in her bed, that she couldn't

move, that something was attacking her—
it was the jungle that had stolen into the
shack and was coiling around her, cover-
ing her in slime and filling her ears with
the unbearable sound of all its creatures
until she herself turned into jungle, into
tree trunk, into moss, into mud, all at the
same time, and then she found her pup,
who licked her face in greeting. When
Damaris awoke she was still alone. Outside
a fierce storm lashed down, wind whipped
against the wood planks, thunder shook
the ground, water streamed through cracks
and floated into the shack.

She thought of Rogelio, out on his mis-
erable boat in the fury of this awful storm
with nothing but a life vest, a rain slicker,
and some plastic sheeting for protection,
but worried more about the pup, out in the
jungle, soaking wet, frozen stiff, scared to
death without Damaris there to save her,
and she wept again.

THE NEXT DAY the storm had passed by midmorning, and Damaris kept searching for the dogs. The day was dark and cool and it had rained so much that everything was flooded. Walking through the water, she returned to the places she'd been the night before, but the downpour had erased all sign of the dogs. Nor was there any sign of them on the main road, which was as flooded as everything else, and she walked the whole length of it. She stopped by the neighbors' to let them know and ask them to keep an eye out: the engineer's caretakers, who were townsfolk and gave the matter no importance; and the Tuluá sisters, who, since they had a lab they adored, shared in Damaris's anguish and asked her to stay to lunch.

In the afternoon she went to see Señora Rosa, who had little to do since Señor Gene's death and had since gotten worse in the head. Before her husband's death Señora Rosa forgot names, lost things, and did stuff that people found funny, like applying her eyeliner or lipstick twice, or putting her cell phone in the freezer. When Señor Gene died, her condition deteriorated. She no longer knew what year it was, thought she was still single in Cali and would start dancing to the national anthem, or thought she and her husband had just moved to the bluff and were awaiting the materials to build their house. She started getting lost on the grounds of her own property, left her mouth hanging open, gawping like an idiot for long stretches of time, talked to the walls, and even forgot to drink, she who so loved liquor and drank almost every day.

Since they had no children, one of her nieces came for her and took charge of everything. She had her admitted to an old folks' home in Cali and put the property up for sale. While waiting for it to sell, the niece continued to pay Damaris and Rogelio to take care of the place, just as her aunt had done. Rogelio took care of the grounds and did repairs, and Damaris cleaned the house.

The pup had gone with Damaris to that property every week since she'd been on the bluff, and suddenly it struck her that the dog might be in her favorite spot, the spot where she liked to lie on the back patio's concrete slab, which stayed cool and dry no matter the weather.

The dog wasn't there, or anyplace else on the property, which was the biggest one on the bluff. Damaris searched the whole of it: the house, the grounds, the steps at the entry, the long ridge of the bluff itself, the path down to the arroyo and even the arroyo itself, which because it had rained so much now cascaded down, spilling over the retaining wall the late Señor Gene had built.

The second day the sun didn't come out either, and it rained hard until midday. Damaris went out after lunch, in drizzle so light she couldn't see or feel it on her skin, though it did get her wet, and she traversed all the minor back trails, the ones only used by hunters and sawyers. Still she saw no sign of the dogs. By midafternoon the rain had stopped, but the sky didn't clear and the day remained gray and cold.

On her way back she came across an ant invasion, thousands and thousands of them advancing through the jungle like an army. They were black medium-sized ants that emerged from their underground nests and dragged off every bug they could find, dead or alive. She had to run to make it past them, but some managed to climb onto her and bit her hands and feet as she shook them off. Though the bites stung like fire, the pain faded quickly and left no welts.

The invasion reached the shack fifteen minutes after she did, and Damaris climbed onto a plastic chair and drew her legs up while they carried out their work cleaning the place. Two hours later there was no sign of the ants, or the cockroaches they'd extracted from their hiding places and taken with them.

That night the temperature dropped so

much Damaris had to cover herself with a towel, the heaviest thing they had in the shack. But still it did not rain. On the third day the sun managed to break through the clouds, the sky and sea filled with color, and it began to warm up. Just as Damaris was about to set out, Rogelio arrived, and, a few minutes later, coming from the direction of the jungle, the dogs made their entrance. They were filthy, exhausted, and a little skinnier. Damaris got excited, but then suddenly saw that it was only Danger, Olivo, and Mosco, and burst into tears.

Though Rogelio had returned hungry and worn out after five days at high sea, he accompanied her into the jungle. They found traces of the three dogs on the main trail and followed them to La Despensa, where the bluff ended and there was another inlet the dogs must have swum across. There was no trace of her pup.

Rogelio kept going out with her every day. They went beyond La Despensa and the fish farm and snuck onto the navy's land, where trespassing was prohibited.

The jungle there turned darker and more mysterious, with tree trunks wide as three Damarises together and the ground so thick with leaves they sometimes came halfway up their boots.

They went out after lunch, and returned in the late afternoon or evening, dead tired, bodies aching from the exertion, scratched by pampas grass, stung by insects, and sweat-covered or drenched when it rained.

One day Damaris realized—on her own, without Rogelio pressuring her or making any discouraging comments—that they were never going to find her dog. They were standing before an enormous hole in the ground where the sea rushed in. The tide was high, waves crashed furiously into the rocks, and they were getting splashed by spray shooting up. Rogelio was telling her that in order to make it across they'd have to wait until tide was as low as possible, climb down into the hole and then go up the rockface on the other side, taking care not to slip since the craggy rocks were covered in slime. Damaris wasn't listening. She was back in the time and place where

Nicolasito had died, and closed her eyes in distress. Then Rogelio was saying they could also try to get around the hole, hack a path with machetes, but the problem was that the other side was full of spiny palms. Damaris opened her eyes and interrupted him.

"The dog's dead," she said.

Rogelio stared at her uncomprehendingly.

"This jungle is horrible," she explained.

There were too many cliffs and bluffs with slime-covered rocks and waves like the one that had carried off the late Nicolasito, enormous trees that storms felled at the root and lightning split down the middle, landslides, snakes that were venomous and others that could swallow a deer, bloodsucking bats that bled animals dry, plants with thorns that could slice through a foot, and arroyos that swelled in the storms and swept off everything in their path ... If that wasn't enough, it had been twenty days since the dog had run off, and that was too long.

"Let's go home," Damaris said, for once without crying.

Rogelio went to her and looked at her; moved, he put a hand on her shoulder. That night they got home and immediately had sex, and it was as if ten years hadn't passed since the last time. Damaris allowed herself to think that maybe this time she'd get pregnant, but the following morning she laughed at herself; she was over forty now, the age women dry up.

Her uncle had said that at one of the parties he threw back when they lived in the two-story house in town. He was drunk and shirtless, sitting outside the house with a group of fishermen, when a woman from town walked by. She was tall and walked proud, swishing her hips, and her hair, which was straightened, reached halfway down her back. Damaris had always admired her. All the fishermen gazed after the woman and her uncle took a drink.

"That is still one fine woman," he said, "and she must by forty by now, the age women dry up."

I was dried up from the start, Damaris thought now, bitter.

For a few days she and Rogelio remained

united. She told him what was happening on the afternoon novelas and he told her what he'd seen or thought about while he hunted, fished, or cut grass. They reminisced about the past, laughed, commented on the news and the evening novela, and slept together like they had back when she was eighteen and hadn't yet started to suffer from not falling pregnant.

One morning, as she was making breakfast in the gazebo, one of the cups Rogelio had bought on his last trip to Buenaventura slipped from Damaris's hands.

"Not even two months," he said, annoyed. "Butterfingers, that's what you've got."

Damaris said nothing in reply, but that night when they turned off the TV and he tried to get with her, she gave him the slip and went into the room where she slept alone. For some time, she gazed at her hands. They were enormous, thick-fingered, with dry, weathered palms and lines deep as cracks in the earth. Man's hands, construction-worker hands or fisherman hands, good for reeling in huge fish. The next day neither of them said good morning and they became distant once more, stopped looking each other in the eye, slept apart, and spoke only when necessary.

DAMARIS STOPPED CRYING over the pup but her absence hurt, like a heavy stone upon her chest; she missed her all the time. When getting back from town and she wasn't there waiting at the top of the steps wagging her tail, when preparing fish and she didn't turn up to stare intently at Damaris, when putting away leftovers and there was no reason to set aside the best for her, and when drinking coffee in the morning and there was nobody's head to scratch. Many a time Damaris thought she saw her: in a cluster of coconuts Rogelio had leaned against the shack, in the mooring lines he left coiled in the gazebo, in a new cord of wood he put by the wood stove, in other dogs, garden plants, tree shadows in the afternoon, and on her little dog bed, which was still in the gazebo exactly the way the pup had left it, since Damaris didn't have the presence of mind to throw it away.

Don Jaime told her he was very sorry, as though a relative had died, and Damaris was grateful to him for taking her feelings seriously. But with Doña Elodia, as she recounted what had happened, Damaris began to feel guilty for having allowed the dog to escape, for not having kept up the search, for having lost hope. Doña Elodia listened in silence and then sighed, as though resigned to life. Her dog was the only one left from a litter of eleven, and now, when going to the next town, Damaris avoided passing the restaurant because it pained her to see him.

Since the last thing she needed right then was to hear Luzmila's negative remarks, Damaris didn't say anything to anyone in her family, not even Tía Gilma. But Luzmila found out regardless. One afternoon, when Rogelio got back from fishing, he bumped into Luzmila's husband at the fisherman's cooperative and, just for something to say, told him the whole story of the dog, her disappearance, and how much they'd searched for her. That night Luzmila called Damaris on her cell.

"That's why I don't like those animals," she said.

Damaris wasn't sure if it was because they might get lost in the jungle or because they died, but instead of asking her to explain she simply asked whether she'd spoken to her father that week.

SEÑOR GENE'S DEATH was very mysterious. No one ever found out what happened to him or how he'd ended up in the sea. By that time he was almost completely paralyzed by his illness and could move only his fingers. Most people believed he'd committed suicide by throwing himself from his wheelchair over the bluff, but Damaris and Rogelio knew that was impossible. The chair's motor wasn't strong enough and, had he tried, Señor Gene would have ended up in the icaco shrubs growing below the ridge, like he did once when he didn't brake in time and Rogelio had had to lift him out with his arms. There was another group who thought Señora Rosa had pushed him—some said out of pity, and others to get rid of him.

Rogelio thought it was possible that Señora Rosa had pushed him, since by then she was already not right in the head. While that last part was true, Damaris was sure that no matter how gaga she might be, it hadn't been her. Señora Rosa didn't hurt the field mice that nested in her pantry, the grasshoppers that ate her clothes, or the enormous moths that looked more like bats and scared her at night, so there was no way she would kill her husband.

In any case, when Señor Gene went missing in his wheelchair and they found no sign of him on the bluff, Rogelio was the first to say that he couldn't be anywhere on earth. The townsmen helping with the search didn't understand.

"If he was anywhere up here," Rogelio explained, casting a glance at the sky, "this whole place would be full of vultures."

It was so true that the men looked at one another as if to say "Why didn't we think of that?" and Damaris felt proud of her husband.

Damaris saw Señor Gene's body right after they pulled it from the sea and brought him to the beach. He looked even whiter than when he was alive, and he'd been *white*-white, the whitest white man Damaris had ever met. His skin was peeled back like an orange in some places, his fingers and toes eaten away by animals, his eye sockets empty, his belly swollen, and his mouth open. Damaris looked inside. His tongue was gone and black water filled his throat. He smelled rotten and she thought that at any moment fish might come up from his belly or vines sprout from his mouth.

Señor Gene had been missing for twenty-one days, the second-longest time the sea had ever taken to return a body, after Nicolasito.

After everyone had stopped asking Damaris about the dog, the dog turned up. Damaris woke early that day to the ruckus of fishing boats heading out to open sea through the cove, where they were moored at night. It was overcast but not raining, and Damaris was worried because they only had one fish to eat. The second she opened the door to go out to the gazebo, she saw the dog in the yard, by the coconut palm. Damaris's first thought was that her eyes were deceiving her yet again, but this time it really was her pup, looking very skinny and covered in mud.

Damaris came out of the shack. The dog began wagging her tail, and Damaris cried once more. She rushed to the dog and crouched down to embrace her. She stank. Damaris examined her. She had ticks, a cut on her ear, a deep gouge on one back paw, and her ribs were sticking out. Damaris stared and stared. She couldn't believe her pup had come back, especially in such good shape after so long in the jungle. It had been thirty-three days, twelve more than Señor Gene had been missing and only one less than Nicolasito, but since it was the jungle that had returned her and not the sea, she was alive. Alive! Damaris couldn't stop repeating it in her head.

"She's alive!" she said out loud, when Rogelio emerged from the shack.

He was so shocked to see the dog he couldn't say a word.

"It's Chirli!" Damaris exclaimed.

"I can see that," he replied.

He walked over, examined her head to tail and even gave her a welcome pat on the haunch. Then he grabbed his shotgun and set off to the jungle to hunt.

Damaris cleaned the dog up, disinfected her wounds with alcohol, and made a fish soup that she served her with the head, leaving herself with nothing to eat. Then she went down to town and in shame asked Don Jaime, who they'd been unable to repay that month, to loan her enough money for Gusantrex, an ointment to keep the dog from getting worms. Don Jaime gave her the money without saying a word and even sold her a pound of rice and two pieces of chicken on credit.

Since it was impossible to get Gusantrex in either of the two towns, Damaris had Luzmila's older daughter arrange for it to be sent from Buenaventura, where she was headed that day, and Damaris didn't even worry about what her cousin might think or say.

The Gusantrex arrived on the very last

boat, and Damaris spent the following days smearing the dog's wounds with ointment, feeding her soup, and pampering her.

THE DOG'S WOUNDS healed and she gained weight, but Damaris continued to treat her as if she was frail, and she no longer cared about calling her Chirli or pampering her in front of anybody, not even when Luzmila came to celebrate Mother's Day.

Luzmila turned up with the entire family—husband, daughters, son-in-law, granddaughters, even Tía Gilma, who they carried up the steps and deposited in one of the lounge chairs on the big house veranda. They made chicken sancocho on the wood stove in the gazebo, filled the pool, and went swimming. Nobody said "Look how brazen we are!" but Damaris felt they must all be thinking it, and even though she laughed at their jokes and played with the girls, she wasn't having a good time. She was mortified at what people would think if they could see them right at that moment, using the Reyeses' house. Tía Gilma was fanning herself on the veranda lounge chair like a queen, Rogelio was lying in the other one by the pool, Luzmila and her husband sat at the pool edge drinking from a bottle of booze, the girls were doing pirouettes in the water, and Damaris, who'd just gotten out, dripped a trail of water behind her all down the pebbled path, her giant bottom in legging shorts and the sleeveless blouse she wore for swimming and work. Nobody would ever mistake them for the owners, Damaris thought to herself. A band of poor, badly dressed black folks using rich people's things. Uppity, that's what people would think, and Damaris wanted to die, because as far as she was concerned being uppity was just as bad and as wrong as committing incest or a crime.

She sat on the ground, legs stretched out, and leaned against the gazebo wall. The pup lay beside her and rested her head on Damaris's thigh, and Damaris began to stroke her. Luzmila watched, shaking her head, then went over to offer Rogelio a drink.

"You get kicked out of bed to make room for that dog?" she asked. "That's who she served the best helping to at lunch."

Luzmila was exaggerating. It's true Damaris had given the dog a dish of sancocho, but it was just skin and a tiny piece of chicken.

"Not yet," Rogelio responded, "but I don't know why she's wasting her time on an animal that got a taste for the jungle and ran off. I told her she's going to keep running away."

ROGELIO WAS RIGHT. Her dog ran away again one day while they were at Señora Rosa's. Damaris left her out on the back patio like always and went up into the house. She opened the windows and doors to air the place out, wiped cobwebs from the corners and dusted the furniture, cleaned the kitchen and bathroom, swept and waxed the floors, and sprayed all the rooms for bugs. Her hands ended up shriveled and smelling of chemicals.

When Damaris finished and came out of the house, around four in the afternoon, the dog wasn't there. There was a thick layer of clouds, so low it was as if they were crushing the earth. The air felt heavy and she assumed that, hot and afraid of the coming rain, the dog had gone home.

Damaris went straight back to find her, wanting to give her a little water. The other dogs had their tongues hanging out and were underneath the shack. Not hers. Damaris couldn't find the pup anywhere. She searched under the big house, the steps, the garden, the gazebo ... Damaris was sweating and stifled by the heat. She wanted to throw water over herself at the sink to cool off, but finding the dog was more important. She called her, shouting from every place on the property, and went a little way into the scrub to keep calling and searching. Damaris kept on until it got too dark to be out barefoot without a flashlight. No luck.

Once back home, she bathed in the washtub. She felt more angry than worried. It infuriated her that the dog had taken off, that she'd done it alone this time, without being influenced by the others, that she'd forced Damaris to shout and search for her, made her suffer and, more than anything else, that Rogelio was right and the dog had turned bad. That was why she didn't say anything when he came back from fishing with a string of fish, and to keep him from figuring it out, she didn't look for her anymore that night. She was so mad she couldn't pay attention to her nightly novela. When she decided to take one last look, the news was already on, and she excused herself saying she had to check and make sure the fish he'd brought were put away properly.

The clouds had moved out and the night was cool and clear. In the distance, over the sea, so far out that she couldn't hear it, was an electrical storm, orange and blue flashes of lightning falling like spiderwebs over the darkness. The dog had come back. She was in her bed, and Damaris was happy to see her but didn't show it.

"Tsssst! Bad girl!" Damaris said when she got up to greet her.

The dog bowed her head and tucked her tail.

"No dinner for you tonight," she threatened.

But she changed her mind in no time and gave her the leftovers she'd set aside.

The following morning the pup was especially docile and didn't leave Damaris's side for a second. Damaris forgave her and decided that Rogelio had been wrong and there was hope for her yet. She took one of the mooring lines Rogelio used to secure the boats, slipped it around her neck using the same knot he used for the canoe, tied her to one of the gazebo's posts, sat next to her, and waited patiently for the dog to try and run off.

As soon as she did, starting to pull, Damaris began speaking in a gentle tone to calm her down, telling her all the things she expected from her: not to run off ever again, to go back to being a good girl, to remember how hungry she'd been and how awful things were those thirty-three days she was lost in the jungle, to not be stubborn, and to learn from her experience. Just then Rogelio returned from the jungle with some wood he needed to repair the shack and looked on the scene in alarm.

"You trying to kill that thing?!" he asked.

"Why do you say that?"

"That's a slipknot: you're going to strangle her!"

Damaris rushed to the dog's neck, intending to free her, but she'd been thrashing desperately so the knot had pulled tight and wouldn't budge. Rogelio pushed Damaris aside, grabbed the dog, held her to the ground and pulled out his machete. Damaris was horrified but before she could react Rogelio cut the rope and the pup was freed.

After the dog had calmed down and drunk some water, Rogelio taught Damaris how to tie her. It was okay to use a slip-knot to keep her from getting free, but not around the neck. Instead, the rope had to go across her chest and over one shoulder and the opposite front leg, the way people wore purses.

DAMARIS KEPT THE dog tied up for a week. It was a long rope, so as the sun advanced she could follow the shade, and also get to the grass outside the gazebo to do her business. Damaris filled her water bowl whenever it was empty and fed her next to the post she was tied to. At night she left the light on, as she always had, to keep the bats from biting her.

At the end of the week, before untying her, Damaris looked into her eyes and said, "I'm watching." The dog bolted like a wild horse and Damaris thought she was going to take off. She didn't. Once she'd tired herself out the dog returned to the gazebo with her tongue hanging out, drank water, and sprawled next to Damaris. This seemed like a good sign, but Damaris remained vigilant regardless. She didn't let her out of sight and when the dog got too far, Damaris called her back to her side; she tied her up at night, when she went to town, and when she was too busy to keep watch.

But it wasn't until she let her guard down a bit, faith restored, that the dog ran away again. This time she was gone one day and one night, and from that point on nothing worked—not tying her up for a whole month or leaving her free the whole time, spending every waking moment on vigil or paying no attention whatsoever, taking away her food as punishment or feeding her extra, being mean to her or smothering her with affection. At the slightest opportunity, the dog was off and would be gone for hours or days.

Rogelio said nothing, but Damaris couldn't stand the idea of him thinking "I told you so" and started to resent the dog. During one of the dog's absences she took her bed from the gazebo and hurled it over the bluff onto a dump in the cove where people threw cans of motor oil and broken gasoline drums. She stopped petting her, saving her the best leftovers, paying attention to her when she wagged her tail, saying goodnight, even leaving the gazebo light on. When the dog got bitten by a bat, Damaris only realized after Rogelio pointed to the trail of blood and asked if she was going to treat it. The cut was on her nose and it bled and bled. When Damaris shrugged and kept on with what she was doing, which was brewing the morning coffee, Rogelio went to the shack for the Gusantrex and applied it himself.

The cut healed fine, and from then on it was Rogelio who made sure to leave the light in the gazebo on at night. It's not that he took over caring for her, but anyone who didn't know them would have thought the dog belonged to him and Damaris was the one who didn't like animals. She started to feel annoyed by the dog's presence, her smell, her scratching and shaking off, the slobber hanging from her muzzle, and, on rainy days, the mud tracks she left on the gazebo floor and the footpaths by the pool and garden. She wanted her to hurry up and leave, not come back, get bitten by a lancehead and die.

But instead she stopped running away and calmed down. She spent her days with Damaris, wherever she was: lying in the gazebo as she cooked or folded clean clothes, under the big house when she cleaned it and under the shack while she watched her afternoon novelas. One day Damaris found herself stroking her like in the old days.

"So beautiful, my little dog," she said so that Rogelio would hear. "Finally came to her senses."

It was late afternoon and she and the dog were sitting on the top step, facing the cove as tide came in, quick, dark, and silent as a giant anaconda. Rogelio was sitting on a plastic chair he'd dragged out of the shack, cleaning his fingernails with a kitchen knife.

"That's just because she's pregnant," he said.

Damaris felt as if she'd been punched in the gut: she couldn't breathe. Couldn't even refuse to accept it because it was so obvious. The pup's teats were swollen and her belly round and firm. It was unbelievable he'd even had to say it.

Damaris was engulfed in sadness, and everything—getting out of bed, making lunch, chewing her food—seemed to require a mammoth effort. She felt that life was like the cove and her lot was to walk across it, feet buried in the mud, water up to her waist, alone, totally alone, in a body that bore her no children and was good only for breaking things.

Damaris barely left the shack. She spent all day shut in watching television on a mat she laid out on the floor; outside, meanwhile, the sea swelled and receded; the rain poured down on the world; and the jungle, so menacing, was all around her without comforting her, like her husband, who slept in another room and didn't ask what was the matter, and her cousin who only came over to criticize her, and her mother who'd gone to Buenaventura and then died, and the pup, who she'd raised only to be abandoned by her.

Damaris couldn't stand the sight of her. It was torture, seeing her ever-expanding belly when she opened the front door. The pup was set on being there all the time, following her from the shack to the gazebo, the gazebo to the washbasin, the washbasin to the shack. Damaris tried to scare her off. "Scat!" she'd say. "Get!" And one time she even raised a hand as though to hit her, but the dog didn't so much as flinch and only stood there right behind her, slow and heavy with the puppies she was carrying inside.

It rained hard that night, but inside the shack it was hot. The electricity had gone out so they were in the dark with no television and the living room full of mosquitos. Rogelio had forgotten to gather coconut jute and they had no way to scare them off. Tormented by the bugs, Damaris wrapped herself head to toe in a sheet. She sat down on one of the plastic chairs by the window, which she didn't open so the water wouldn't get in, and listened to the constant drone of the rain, like people praying at a wake. Rogelio put on his slicker and boots and walked out of the shack saying he'd rather be in the gazebo, where at least there were no walls and he could cool off in the rain's mist. He hadn't been gone long when the door flew open. There stood Rogelio, no slicker and soaking wet.

"The puppies are being born!" he cried.

Damaris remained rooted to her spot at the window.

"And you think I care?" she asked.

"Boy, are you bitter. Isn't she your dog? I thought you loved her so much."

She said nothing in reply and Rogelio left.

Damaris saw the puppies the next day when she got hungry and had to go out to the gazebo to make lunch. Rogelio had improvised a bed using his slicker, and the dog was suckling them. There were four in all, each with different coats and as tiny, blind, and helpless as the pup herself had been the day Damaris first saw her at Doña

Elodia's. They smelled of milk, and Damaris couldn't resist. She picked them up one by one, brought them to her nose so she could inhale their scent, and pressed them to her bosom.

The dog turned out to be a horrible mother. On the second night she ate one of her puppies and in the days that followed abandoned the remaining three so she could go lie in the sun by the pool or sprawl in the washtub, where it was always cool, or under one of the houses with the other dogs—anything not to be with them. Damaris had no choice but to grab the dog, carry her back to the gazebo, and force her to lie down so they could suckle.

When they were two weeks old Damaris had to go buy powdered milk because the dog didn't feed them enough and they yowled day and night in hunger. They weren't even a month old when she ran away yet again, and when she didn't come back they had to learn to eat leftovers. By the time the dog returned, several days later, her milk had dried up and she shunned them completely.

The puppies did their business in the gazebo, on the footpaths, the steps, everywhere but on the grass, and now Damaris, in addition to all her other chores, had to chase after them cleaning up their mess. One day when she went to clean Señora Rosa's and was gone all afternoon, Rogelio came back from fishing and stepped in a pile of it, and though he was wearing flip-flops and only the soles got mess on them, he was furious and shouted, saying the next time he wouldn't be accountable for his actions.

Rogelio didn't step in any more mess, but a few days later one of the puppies jumped on him and bit his feet with its tiny needle teeth, and he kicked it so hard it slammed into the gazebo wall.

"Monster!" Damaris screamed and went to tend to the puppy. It was the girl, the most playful of them all, a little ball of black fur with a white patch on one eye.

Rogelio kept walking without apologizing or even turning to see what had happened. Though the puppy had hit the wall hard and was stunned, she recovered

quickly and a few minutes later was playing once more.

The following day Damaris set about to
find them homes.

AT THE TOURIST cabins on the hill leading up to the next town they wanted the biggest one, a boy dog with red hair and long ears. And the second boy dog, gray and short-haired like his mother, was adopted by one of Don Jaime's wife's sisters. Nobody wanted the girl. There was no vet in the area, no way to sterilize animals, and nobody wanted to be responsible for a bitch in heat, much less her puppies. Often, from the bluff, Damaris had seen people throw a whole litter of puppies or kittens into the cove to be swept away by the tides.

Doña Elodia was helping with the search and reminded Damaris about Ximena, who'd lost her dog and had wanted a girl from the start anyway. Neither one of them, nor anyone they knew, had Ximena's cell phone number, so Damaris went to her handicraft stall in the next town to ask if she was interested.

Ximena said yes, excited, and they agreed she'd come and pick the puppy up the next day. Since she didn't know the way to the bluff, Damaris gave her directions and they exchanged cell phone numbers. She spent all day waiting, but Ximena never showed up. Having no minutes left on her cell phone, Damaris had to wait until the following morning, when tide was out and she was going to town to do the shopping, to make a call using Don Jaime's phone service. Ximena didn't answer, nor did she come for the puppy that afternoon or in the days that followed.

Another week went by. The puppy was at a terrible age. She demanded more food than the big dogs, bit Damaris's feet constantly, shat all over the place, and chewed up everything in sight: a chair leg, Damaris's only nice shoes, the kitchen rags, and one of Rogelio's fishing floats, which Damaris tossed over the bluff without telling him so he wouldn't punish the little dog.

When he asked if she'd seen his float, she said no, and he looked at her skeptically but didn't say or do anything.

Damaris was telling herself she saw why people threw puppies into the sea and trying to convince herself that it was what she'd have to do, when a stevedore who worked at the docks approached her in town. He'd heard she was giving puppies away and wanted to know if she had any left. Damaris said there was only one left, a girl.

"How soon could I take her?" he asked, determined.

Damaris thought about calling Ximena to make sure she no longer wanted the puppy, but even though she was close to the dock and there were lots of people around there selling calls on their cell phones, she decided not to. What if Ximena didn't answer and the docker felt bad about taking an animal Damaris had promised someone else? Or, worse yet, what if she did answer, promised she'd come for the puppy like she had before, and then never showed up?

"If you want we can go get her right now," Damaris said.

Tide was out, so they crossed the cove on foot, water up to their ankles. He had never been up to the bluff before. The man's jaw dropped as he admired the pool, the garden and sea view, the islands and cove. But he didn't say a word about the big house.

"The owners haven't sent money for paint or supplies in twenty years," Damaris explained.

"It's a wonder the place is still standing," he said.

She handed him the puppy and off he went, smiling and petting her.

Damaris stood there and watched him from above. He was a very ugly man, pockmarks on his face and so skinny he looked ill, a survivor of every malaria that ever was. His wife was even fatter than Damaris and at least twenty years older than he was, but the two of them always walked through town holding hands. Damaris was sure they'd really love the little puppy, since they didn't have kids either, and she wondered if that was what kept them united.

IT WAS ANOTHER week before Ximena showed up, which was two weeks later than when she'd said she'd come for the puppy. Damaris was in the shack cleaning the bathroom when she heard the dogs barking and went out to see what was going on. The dogs were at the top of the steps, Danger with his hackles raised and growling, Mosco and Olivo on either side, barking as backup. Ximena stood a few meters below, frozen on the top landing. Damaris calmed the dogs, who dispersed, and Ximena climbed the rest of the way up.

It was low tide, she'd walked across the cove and her legs were wet, flipflops and feet covered in mud. And she was flustered and sweaty. It was clear that walking from the next town, crossing the cove, climbing the steps to the bluff, and being startled by the dogs had worn her out. Damaris offered Ximena water but the woman pointed to the backpack crossed over her chest.

"Got some," she said, and then added impatiently, "I'm here for my puppy."

Damaris had bleach on her hands and dried them on her T-shirt. Apologetic, she explained that since Ximena hadn't come to pick the puppy up or answered her phone call, she'd given her away.

"You gave my puppy to someone else?!"

Damaris nodded and Ximena flew into a rage. She claimed this was the limit, that Damaris had given away an animal that wasn't even hers, that the puppy had stopped being hers the moment she'd offered it to Ximena and Ximena had said yes, that Damaris knew very well how much she wanted that dog, how excited she was to take care of her, how she'd already made a little bed for her, arranged for food to be sent in from Buenaventura, and said that at the very least she could have had the courtesy to tell her not to come so she could have saved herself the fucking walk to this shithole that was farther than the last circle of hell.

Damaris responded calmly, saying there was no need to start using foul language, and tried again to explain her reasoning, but Ximena didn't want to hear it or accept her share of the responsibility and interrupted, saying:

"Fine, I'll take a different one."

Damaris fell silent and stared at the ground.

"What?" Ximena said, interpreting correctly, "You don't have any more?"

Damaris shook her head.

"There were only three to begin with, and when I offered you the girl she was the only one left."

Ximena glared, as though attempting with her eyes to cast every hex in creation upon Damaris, who felt that this look was going on far too long.

"You should have called me before giving my puppy away," Ximena finally said.

"I thought about it, but since you didn't answer the other time ..."

"What? You assumed I wouldn't answer this time either?"

Damaris lowered her voice:

"Or that you weren't interested in the puppy anymore."

"You did wrong, you should have called me, you know that."

Damaris said nothing more, since there was no point. Ximena turned to go, and there before her saw the mama dog, just coming up the steps. Lately she'd begun running off not only to the jungle but to town, and despite hating water she'd learned to swim across the cove, even when tide was at its highest. Her paws were muddy and she was dripping. Ximena, who no longer looked angry, glanced at Damaris.

"Is that the mother?" she asked.

"Yes," Damaris said.

"She's so pretty. That's how I pictured mine. How sad to leave empty-handed."

Ximena kept walking. The dog began wagging her tail at Damaris and Damaris abhorred her. She'd been gone a week and now here she was back to cover everything she touched in filth.

THAT NIGHT DAMARIS gazed at the dog with no ill will, and after a while she tied her and actually ran a hand down the length of her, which she hadn't done since before the puppies were born.

The following morning she went down to town with the dog on the rope. Tide was all the way out so they walked across the beach, which was huge and gray, like the sea and sky. The fishermen were out on their boats and the only people on the beach were a few naked children with snotty noses, playing in the trash. It had rained something fierce all night long, but now it was only a light drizzle that didn't keep anyone from going about their business as though it wasn't raining at all. The rain was always so cool and clean it seemed to purify the world, but it was actually the reason that moss and mold covered everything: tree trunks, the pier's cement columns, lampposts, the houses' wooden stilts and wallboards, and their zinc and asbestos roofs.

As they made their way along, strays emerged from under houses and restaurants, trotting over to sniff the pup, and to Damaris's dismay, she wagged her tail at them all, proving that she knew them. Damaris was relieved to see that Doña Elodia wasn't at the restaurant, for she wouldn't have known how to explain what she was about to do.

They left the beach, walked down the paved street, made their way past a row of houses, shops, and small wooden hotels, less decadent than the ones on the beach with lacquered or brightly painted fronts and orchid-filled gardens, walked across the military airport and Whale Park, where at the right time of year you could see whales jump, and reached the next town.

The sky was still overcast but it had stopped raining, and Ximena was setting up her stall. She arranged her merchandise on the velvet meticulously, as if drawing lines with a ruler. Ximena looked up in surprise as they approached, especially when they stopped in front of her.

"What are you doing here?"

"I came to bring her to you."

"Your little dog?" Ximena asked in shock.

"If you'll accept her," Damaris said.

"Of course I will," Ximena exclaimed excitedly, and crouched down to pet her. "How could I not accept her when she's my little Simoncito's sister?"

Then suddenly she stopped and looked up, regarding Damaris skeptically.

"Why are you giving her to me?"

"Because you love her more than I do."

This explanation seemed to satisfy Ximena.

"You do have too many dogs already," she said, petting her again. "What's her name?"

"Chirli."

"Hewooo, Chirli!" Ximena cooed in baby talk, stroking her head and haunches. "Hewooo, my pwetty wittle girl. How are you?"

The dog wagged her tail.

"You'll have to tie her up," Damaris warned her. "At least till she gets used to things, or she'll run away."

"Obviously," said Ximena.

BUT A FEW days later the dog returned to the house on the bluff. Damaris was watching her novela and had to turn it off and rush out of the shack to shoo her away so the dog wouldn't think she was welcome. Damaris made all sorts of gestures and used threatening voices, but since the dog wasn't afraid of her, all she did was take refuge under the big house. When Damaris tried to force her out with a broom handle, the dog hid in the middle, where even the long handle of the skimmer they used to clean the pool couldn't reach her.

If she'd had any minutes left on her phone, Damaris would have called Ximena and told her to come get the dog, washed her hands of the whole affair, and gone back to her novela. Since she had no minutes, she got all worked up and began insulting Ximena in her head. "Stupid woman," she said. "Didn't I tell you to tie her up? Too many vices to pay attention." She carried on as though Ximena had responded. "Oh, you did tie her up, did you? Well, you did a bad job, you big dummy, you crazy old fool. All that gray hair and wrinkles and you still haven't learned how to tie a damn knot?" Damaris was pacing around the big house wielding the skimmer's long pole in one hand, waving the other in the air and making faces as though she was actually mid-quarrel. Rogelio was out trimming Señora Rosa's grass, but if he'd seen Damaris at that moment he would have thought she'd lost her mind.

Suddenly Damaris knew what she had to do. She dropped the skimmer and left it on the path, went to the washtub, filled the biggest bucket they had, grabbed a shallow gourd, returned to the big house, crouched down as close to where the dog was as possible, and began to throw water at her. Almost none of it hit her, just a few drops, but the dog hated water so much that this was enough to drive her out. The dog ran into the garden, and Damaris waited for her to get distracted and then crept up and dumped the whole bucket on her.

Startled, the poor thing jumped and then looked at Damaris in confusion, or maybe it was in horror, and trotted away from the one person who'd been her ally and had now committed this grave betrayal against her. With her tail between her legs, she kept turning her head and looking back, so as to protect herself from Damaris, who got the feeling that this time she'd broken an irreparable bond between the two of them. Contrary to what she'd expected, it hurt.

That dog had been hers: she'd rescued her, carried her around in her brassiere, taught her to feed, where to do her business, to be good, until she became a full-grown bitch and didn't need her. Damaris followed her all the way through the garden to the steps and watched her trot down, cross the cove—which was dry—get to the other side, shake herself off, make her way through the children coming home from school, and disappear into town without looking back even once. Damaris didn't cry, but almost.

THE FOLLOWING MORNING, the dog was back in the gazebo, lying in the same spot where her bed had been. The second she saw Damaris she got up and moved. When Damaris tried to get close enough to grab her, the dog left the gazebo even though it was raining hard. So Damaris pretended she had no interest in her, hid the rope, lit the fire, and started making coffee without so much as glancing at her.

The dog wasn't going to spend long under the overhang, where the water running off the gazebo roof splashed down and got her wet, when she could be dry and protected inside. The doorway on that side was next to the stove, so Damaris waited patiently for the dog to come in and grabbed her right there, slipping the rope around her neck like a cow. She pulled the slipknot tight to restrain her, which was the only way to get close enough to then loosen the rope and tie it the way Rogelio had shown her, looping it under one leg so the dog wouldn't suffocate.

There had been a huge downpour that night, and though it wasn't raining as hard now, nothing suggested it was going to let up anytime soon. The tide was high and stormy, dragging in sticks and branches. Rogelio had been awake for a while but had yet to emerge from the shack. Seeing Damaris go by with the dog, heading toward the steps, he stuck his head out the window.

"You going out in this?" he asked in astonishment.

Damaris said yes and told him she'd left him his coffee in the gazebo.

"Where to?"

"To drop off the dog and do the shopping."

"Drop her off where?"

"With a woman I gave her to."

"You gave your dog away? What for?"

Rogelio stared at her uncomprehendingly.

She shrugged, and he kept at it with the questions.

"Can't you wait until the storm clears and tide goes out?"

"No," she said.

Rogelio shook his head in disapproval but didn't attempt to dissuade her and stopped trying to find an explanation.

"Bring me four batteries for the flash-light," he said.

Damaris nodded and kept going with the dog. Crossing the cove with her in the canoe would have been impossible so they swam instead, dodging the storm debris. When they reached the other side, Damaris turned back to the bluff. Rogelio was still at the window, watching.

THEY WALKED ALL the way to the next
town in the rain and got there drenched
and shivering. Nobody was out on the arti-
san's street, not Ximena nor any of the
indigenous vendors, so Damaris walked
into the big store a few meters further on.
The young man there, thin with light eyes,
said he thought Ximena lived along Arrastradero, a long inlet that went all the way
down past the next town.

At another store, just before the turnoff
to Arrastradero, Damaris asked again, con-
firming that Ximena lived straight down
the turnoff, in a small blue house on the
left, before the dock. By then the rain had
turned to drizzle, and by the time they got
there it had stopped entirely.

Ximena's house looked fake, like a

dollhouse plopped down in the middle of the mudflat that was the road to Arrastradero. It was freshly painted in bright colors: electric blue walls and a red front door, roof, windows, and porch bannisters. The door was open, reggaetón blasting out at full volume.

Damaris walked up to the porch and could see inside. The kitchen was in the back and opened onto the living room. There was a woman in there stirring something in a pot on the stove. She looked Ximena's age, maybe a little younger, and they resembled one another. In the living room, sprawled on the sofa, were two kids from town, black, shirtless, and barefoot. One was in his underwear and had braids and the other had a shaved head, cutoffs, and bling around his neck. Ximena sat facing them on a wooden bench, a beer in one hand and a cigarette in the other. Her head was bowed and her hair unkempt. It was only about nine in the morning and all of them looked drunk or high or both.

"Good morning," Damaris called. Nobody heard her. "Yoo hoo," she tried, louder.

The kid in his underwear turned and Damaris recognized him. He was one of Doña Elodia's grandkids. He got Ximena's attention and she looked at the door, eyes bleary, and registered the presence of Damaris and the dog. Stubbing her cigarette out in an ashtray overflowing with butts, she got up and started stumbling toward her, light on her feet, as if she was about to take off and fly any second. When she made it to the door, she grabbed on for support.

"My little doggie," she said, thick-tongued. "You're not going to tell me you walked all the way here from your house?"

"That is what I'm going to tell you."

"I left the door open by mistake, just for one little second, and she got out."

"She's been at my house since yesterday afternoon."

"I was going to come and get her, but my friends came to visit."

Ximena gestured toward the boys.

"This dog is your responsibility."

"I know."

"Tie her, lock her up, keep the door

closed, do whatever you have to do, but don't let her run away."

"I won't."

"I hope there's not a next time, but if there is, I'm not bringing her back to you."

Ximena was docile and complacent when drunk, nothing like the feisty scrapper she was when sober.

"Don't you fret, I'll take care of her," she said.

Damaris held out the rope. Ximena took it and crouched down intending to pet the dog but ended up falling to the floor. The last thing Damaris saw before heading back down the road was Ximena on the floor, legs akimbo like a ragdoll, and the pup with her tail between her legs, her face turned to Damaris, staring in distress as though she'd been left at the slaughter-house.

DAMARIS STOPPED OFF at Don Jaime's shop to buy minutes for her phone, batteries for her flashlight as well as Rogelio's, and lots of groceries. They'd been given their caretaker wages for Señora Rosa's that week, and Rogelio had caught a ton of fish using his drift net and sold them to the co-op at a good price, which meant she could buy everything outright as well as repay everything they owed with a few damp bills she pulled from her brassiere, and still have a bit left that for the following week's groceries.

Damaris spent the night cooking. She fried lots of fish and made soup, rice, and salad. Then she set some aside for their breakfast and her lunch the next day and packed the rest for Rogelio, who was going out on a wind-and-tide. The long boat was already docked, its rigging all set, ready to be boarded. Damaris felt happy. There was a chance Rogelio would be gone several days and she was looking forward to the time alone.

He left before sun up, and Damaris slept in. She didn't do anything that day. Since she'd already cooked there wasn't even any need to make lunch. Damaris laid her mat in the living room and stretched out to watch TV. She didn't shower and only got up to go to the bathroom, to eat, and to feed the dogs when they stationed themselves at the door and stared at her persistently. She ate straight from the pots, masturbated twice—once in the morning and again in the late afternoon—and watched all of the novelas, newscasts, and reality shows that were on until it got dark and a terrible storm with hurricane winds and lightning that struck too close hit, the power went out, and she fell asleep.

The following day there was no sign of the storm. Damaris woke up feeling energetic, decided to do a thorough cleaning of the big house and put on her spandex shorts and the faded sleeveless blouse she used as a work shirt. In the morning she concentrated on the bathroom and the kitchen. She emptied out all of the cabinets and drawers to do an in-depth clean, washed all the plates and glasses, silverware and other kitchen utensils, cleaned the windows and mirror, scrubbed the kitchen sink, shower, bathroom sink, floors and walls, and bleached the floor tiles and even the grout between them. A few of the tiles were chipped, the mirror had little black moisture stains all over it, and there were rust stains in both sinks, but aside from that everything was gleaming and Damaris looked over her work with satisfaction.

It was lunchtime so she went to the gazebo to make her favorite meal: rice, one fried egg, sliced tomato with salt, and fried green plantain. She ate slowly, gazing out at the sea, which was calm and blue after the storm. Damaris started thinking about the Reyeses, who would have to return at some point, and she hoped would do so on a day like this, to see the big house in the process of being cleaned and her sweating and filthy in her spandex shorts and sleeveless work blouse, so they'd realize that even though they weren't paying her a cent she was a good worker, a good person.

She thought about the late Nicolasito, his laugh, his face, the somersaults he used to do in the pool. The day they made a deal and shook hands, all serious, like they were adults, and the time he told her that the animals and boy on the curtains and sheets in his room came from his favorite movie, which was called *The Jungle Book* and was also a book, about a boy who gets lost in the jungle and then saved by the animals. "He gets saved by animals?" Damaris asked, confused, and when Nicolasito said yes, by a panther and a family of wolves, Damaris burst out laughing because that was impossible.

Even though they seemed happy, these memories were terrible, because they always brought her back to the same place: Nicolasito, slender and white, out on the bluff. "Damn that wave for taking him away," she said to herself. No, damn her for not stopping him, not preventing it, for standing there without doing anything, even screaming.

Damaris felt the weight of blame once more, as though time had not passed. The Reyeses' suffering, her uncle whipping her, the looks she got from people who knew that she—who knew the bluff and its dangers—could have avoided the tragedy, and Luzmila's words a few months later when, before going to sleep, in the dark of night, she insinuated that Damaris had been jealous of Nicolasito. "Cause he had those swamp boots," she'd said. Damaris was furious: "You're the one who was jealous of him," she said, and refused to speak to her cousin until she'd apologized.

Now Damaris stared blankly at the polished cement floor for a moment, thinking about her mother, the day she went off to Buenaventura and left her with Tío Eliécer. Damaris was four years old, wearing a hand-me-down dress that was too small and had two braids sticking out of her head like antennae. Back then there were no speedboats or dock, just a boat that came once a week, which people boarded from canoes that rowed out to it from the beach. Damaris and her uncle were on the shore and her mother stood in line where the waves broke, her pants rolled up. No doubt she was about to step into the canoe that would take her to the boat, but the image stored in Damaris's memory was one of her mother walking out to the sea until she disappeared from sight. It was one of her first memories and always made Damaris feel lonely, and cry.

She wiped her tears and got up. She washed the dishes and went back to the big house to continue working. After taking down the curtains in the living room and bedrooms, she carried them out to the gazebo and set the ones from the late Nicolasito's room to one side because she always washed them separately, more carefully and gently. Washing curtains was hard work and took muscle and grit, especially the ones from the living room, which were enormous since they covered a picture window that went from floor to ceiling and wall to wall. The washtub wasn't very big and she had to wash the curtains section by section, her back hunched and hands scrubbing hard, over and over, until the suds got the grime out and the water ran clear; she did this on each section of the curtain, her back aching, her awkward man-hands scrubbing nonstop, thinking that she wasn't being paid to do this, thinking that it was true she'd been jealous of Nicolasito, though not for his swamp boots or the nice things he had—the new shirts, the toys that Baby Jesus brought him, the matching *Jungle Book* curtains and bed set—but the fact that he lived with his parents: Señor Luis Alfredo, who used to say "Let's wrestle, champ" and always let him win; and Señora Elvira, who smiled when she saw him come home and ran her hand through his hair to straighten it. And she told herself that she deserved all the dirty looks people gave her, all the suspicion and accusations, and the lashes she'd gotten from Tío Eliécer, who should have hit her more times and with more fury.

By the time she'd finished there was little

left of the dwindling afternoon and she was beat. The sea was still as calm as a vast, never-ending swimming pool but Damaris was not deceived. She knew full well that this was the same evil beast that swallowed people up and spat them out. She bathed in the washtub, hung the curtains out to dry on the clotheslines in the gazebo, and ate the rice left in the pot. Damaris realized she hadn't seen the dogs and looked for them to feed them but couldn't find them anywhere. Then she returned to the shack and, without so much as changing out of her work clothes, lay on the mat in front of the television thinking she'd have a little rest, but in the middle of her novela she fell into a deep sleep, calm as death, that lasted till the following morning.

IT HADN'T RAINED and it was beautiful out that morning. Damaris turned off the TV, which had been on all night, opened the windows to let in the sun, and went out to the gazebo with the intention of making herself some coffee. What she found there left her horrorstruck. The late Nicolasito's curtains were on the ground, muddy and torn. Damaris crouched to pick them up and a piece came off in her hand. They were so ripped up it would be impossible to mend them. Nicolasito's *Jungle Book* curtains!

Then she saw the dog. She was at the back of the gazebo, lying next to the woodfire stove behind the other curtains, which she hadn't touched and were still hanging. Livid, Damaris grabbed a mooring line, made a slipknot, marched out of the gazebo on the pool side, circled around to come back in on the stove side, and slipped it over the dog's neck from behind before she knew what was going on. Damaris tugged the rope to tighten the knot, but rather than stop, take it off her neck, and loop it under one leg, she kept yanking and yanking, tugging with all her might as the dog thrashed before her eyes, which seemed not to register what they were seeing, registered only the dog's swollen teats.

"Pregnant again," Damaris said to herself, and tugged even harder, tugged and tugged, until long after the dog had surrendered in exhaustion, curled into a ball on the ground, and stopped moving. A yellow pool of strong-smelling urine extended slowly toward Damaris, growing longer and thinner until it reached her bare feet. Only then did Damaris react. She let the rope slacken, stepped away from the puddle, got close enough to nudge the dog with one foot and, when she didn't react, had to accept what she'd done.

Distraught, Damaris dropped the rope

and stared at the dead dog, the thin puddle of urine, and the rope, which was now curled on the floor like a snake. She contemplated it all in horror, but also with a kind of satisfaction best not to acknowledge and instead bury under other emotions. Exhausted, she sat down on the floor.

DAMARIS DIDN'T KNOW how long she sat there. It seemed an eternity. Then she crawled over on all fours to try to loosen the rope around the dog's neck. She couldn't get to it, so after another eternity she stood up, grabbed a big knife, and used that to cut the rope. The dog was freed and Damaris had the urge to pet her but did not. She just stared. The dog looked asleep.

Next she lifted her up in her arms, which ached from the struggle, and carried her to the jungle. Damaris left her deep in the jungle, out past the arroyo, next to the pacay tree, where the ground was covered in leaves and white pulp from the tree's flowers. It was a pretty place that brought back good memories because she, the late Nicolasito, and Luzmila had climbed that tree countless times, searching for fruit. Before returning she gazed at the dog a few moments, as though praying.

Damaris folded the late Nicolasito's ruined curtains and placed them in a plastic bag, which she put in his room, in the wardrobe, with his clothes and the mothballs. The bare window distressed her, and she pictured the Reyeses' reaction when they walked into their dead son's room and realized that the curtains were missing. She thought of Rogelio, too, who would no doubt say something like "What'd you expect? I told you." "Damn dog," she said, going for an old sheet to cover the window. "She deserved it."

Damaris had yet to finish cleaning the big house. She hadn't done the wardrobes, polished the wood floors, or washed the sheets, but she had no spirit to do anything else that day, even cook or eat, and since the dogs hadn't come back she didn't have to feed them either. She lay on her mat and spent another entire day spacing out in front of the TV and was unable to sleep, even well into the night, after it began to rain and the power went out.

It was a powerful storm, but there wasn't any wind so it fell steadily, vertically, down onto the asbestos roof, hammering away and drowning out all other sounds, all other sensations, and Damaris felt like she couldn't take it, not one minute more. She couldn't get what had happened out of her head: the fight the dog put up, her struggling to tighten the rope and overpower the animal, tugging with all her might, tightening the rope until there was no more resistance. So that was what it was to kill. Damaris thought it wasn't hard and didn't even take long.

Then she remembered the woman who'd chopped her husband up with a hatchet and fed the pieces to a tiger, which on the news they called a jaguar. This had been at a reserve in lower San Juan, and the tiger was caged. The woman claimed she hadn't killed her husband, that he'd been bitten by a lancehead and died, and that, since they were so far from anything, with no form of communication, she didn't know what to do with the corpse. She couldn't bury it because in the jungle the ground was clay and so hard it would have been impossible to dig a hole the size she needed, and rather than throw him into the sea or leave him to be eaten by vultures she decided to give him to the tiger, who was always hungry. Nobody believed her. A woman who could chop her husband's body up and feed the pieces to a tiger was so full of fury she must have killed him.

When the police were taking her from San Juan to Buenaventura they made a stop in town on their way, and everyone went to the dock to see her. She was handcuffed, and her hair, which was long and black, fell over her face, though everyone could still see her eyes. They were brown and ordinary, the eyes of any old white lady who in other circumstances no one would have remembered. But her gaze—which she never lowered, and held to anyone who dared face her—was so hard that Damaris had never forgotten it. It was the look of a killer, the same one she herself must have now, the look of someone unrepentant, relieved at having freed themselves of a burden.

Ximena wasn't taking care of the dog, who was pregnant again, and would have kept getting out and coming back to what she considered her home no matter how many times Damaris brought her back there. She'd have ended up giving birth in the gazebo, and yet again it would have fallen to Damaris to take care of the puppies because the dog, proven bad mother that she was, would have abandoned them, and this time who knew how many there'd have been and how many girls nobody would want. And that time she really would have had to throw them into the sea, which was the same as killing them, killing a bunch of dogs and not just one, which had solved the whole problem.

The place Damaris had left her was perfect. It was far from the trails, concealed by dense vegetation, and no one ever went there. When people in town saw the vultures, if they even noticed them at all, they'd think it was some wild animal, an opossum, a deer, or a sloth, like the one that had died that one time out by La Despensa. Besides, in that jungle it would only take three days, four at the most, for the corpse to be reduced to bones that she'd gather and throw into the sea, at night so nobody saw, when tide was going out and would carry them far away. Damaris prayed that Rogelio wouldn't return until after she'd disposed of the remains. "I bet he won't," she thought, optimistically.

And if Ximena asked about the dog, which at some point no doubt she would, Damaris would say she hadn't seen her. "Why?" she'd ask, playing dumb, "how long has she been missing?" "That long?!" she'd exclaim on hearing the reply. "And it took you all this time to come look for her? That's very irresponsible, who knows where that dog could be, what kind of shape she's in; if I'd known you were going to neglect her, I never would have given her to you."

Damaris sincerely hoped none of the people who lived by the cove and knew the dog's gray coat had seen her going up to the bluff that morning, hoped that Ximena wouldn't go and get all mad and insistent the way she had the other day, or worse yet, accuse Damaris as she had the neighbors, who she claimed with no proof at all had poisoned her other dog.

Why had she given that woman her phone number? Damaris chided herself. Why did she say if the dog got out again she wouldn't bring her back? Why insist it was Ximena's responsibility to come get her? The last thing Damaris needed right now was that woman turning up at her house. "There's no way," Damaris thought, calming herself, "she's probably still drunk and high with her boys."

Both the storm and the night began to recede at almost the same time, and once it was completely light Damaris got up. She hadn't slept at all but didn't feel tired. The moment she got to the gazebo the stench of urine hit her, strong and sour: she'd forgotten to clean up the puddle. Rather than make coffee she went to the washtub for detergent and cleaning utensils. She scrubbed the floor on all fours, not just where the pup had peed but the entire gazebo floor, and then she dried it with the mop. She inhaled. The smell hadn't gone at all, Damaris thought, and before cleaning it all over again decided to bathe in case it was her who smelled, since she'd gotten her hands, knees, and spandex shorts wet.

Damaris went out to the washtub and began to pour water over herself with the gourd. She could still smell urine. She scrubbed herself all over with the blue bar of laundry soap, and then rinsed off. The smell wouldn't go. Next she grabbed the rectangular mirror she used when doing her hair or extracting blackheads. She wanted to see if she found, in that mirror, the same look as the woman who'd chopped up her husband, and she thought she did, and that people would be able to tell, and would know what she'd done. Then she gazed at the wide rough hands that had killed a dog with a belly full of puppies and thought she saw rope marks on them. Full of anguish, as though praying to heaven, she gazed upward. The vultures had arrived.

Some were circling the spot where she'd left the dog, others had perched high up on the branches of a dying tree close to the pacay. The ones in the tree were hunched over and looking down as if ready to swoop, just awaiting the signal. There were too many of them, far more than had gathered for the late Josué or the dead sloth. Damaris, wet and smelling of urine, walked from the washtub through the garden to the steps to see if anyone in town had spotted them.

She peered over the bluff but didn't have time to inspect the beach or dock, where people tended to concentrate, or even the houses by the cove, because the first thing her eyes saw was Ximena on the opposite side. Tide was high and Ximena, pants rolled up, was settling herself into a canoe. The rower, one of the fishermen who lived by the cove, began paddling toward the bluff as Ximena talked nonstop. She could have been saying anything—relaying juicy gossip from the next town, or remarking on the marvelous weather that sunny morning—but Damaris sensed that she was telling him about the dog and that the fisherman was responding that he'd seen her going up to the bluff the day before. She wanted to hide, but then he pointed up and they both lifted their heads and stared at the sky, black with vultures. And they saw Damaris, who had no time to hide or do anything else. Ximena raised a hand in what might have been a greeting but which Damaris took as a threatening gesture. She was done for.

At first she considered the possibility of staying put until Ximena got there, considered letting the woman see her killer's hands and expression and notice the smell of urine, considered accepting the blame and the punishment she deserved but then told herself that neither Ximena nor the townsfolk could punish her the way she deserved. So she thought maybe she should head into the jungle, barefoot, in nothing but her spandex shorts and faded sleeveless blouse, and go out past La Despensa, past the fish farm, the navy land, the places she and Rogelio had gone and those that they hadn't, and get lost the way the dog and the boy on Nicolasito's curtains had, out where the jungle was most terrible.

LISA DILLMAN lives in Georgia, USA, where she translates Spanish, Catalan, and Latin American writers and teaches at Emory University. Some of her recent translations include *Such Small Hands* (winner of the 2018 Oxford-Weidenfeld Translation Award) by Andrés Barba; *Signs Preceding the End of the World* (winner of the 2016 Best Translated Book Award), *Kingdom Cons*, and *The Transmigration of Bodies* (shortlisted for the 2018 Dublin Literary Award) by Yuri Herrera; and *Breathing Through the Wound* and *A Million Drops* by Víctor del Árbol.

On the Design

As book design is an integral part of the reading experience, we would like to acknowledge the work of those who shaped the form in which the story is housed.

Tessa van der Waals (Netherlands) is responsible for the cover design, cover typography, and art direction of all World Editions books. She works in the internationally renowned tradition of Dutch Design. Her bright and powerful visual aesthetic maintains a harmony between image and typography and captures the unique atmosphere of each book. She works closely with internationally celebrated photographers, artists, and letter designers. Her work has frequently been awarded prizes for Best Dutch Book Design.

The image on the cover is by Felipe Manorov Gomes, a freelance photographer from Brazil. The location of the photograph is Seixas beach in João Pessoa, the easternmost point of the American continent. Gomes says this particular image—taken on a trip to visit friends—is one of his personal favorites: "The stray dog was standing in the middle of the beach looking toward the ocean while going unnoticed by the people around her. She is gazing at the horizon as if in deep thought, with her mind elsewhere, just like a human."

The cover has been edited by lithographer Bert van der Horst of BFC Graphics (Netherlands).

Suzan Beijer (Netherlands) is responsible for the typography and careful interior book design of all World Editions titles.

The text on the inside covers and the press quotes are set in Circular, designed by Laurenz Brunner (Switzerland) and published by Swiss type foundry Lineto.

All World Editions books are set in the typeface Dolly, specifically designed for book typography. Dolly creates a warm page image perfect for an enjoyable reading experience. This typeface is designed by Underware, a European collective formed by Bas Jacobs (Netherlands), Akiem Helmling (Germany), and Sami Kortemäki (Finland). Underware are also the creators of the World Editions logo, which meets the design requirement that "a strong shape can always be drawn with a toe in the sand."